BEAUTIFULLY UNFIXABLE

CANDIED CRUSH #9

CHARITY PARKERSON

—Warning: This book is intended for readers over the age of 18.

Copyright © 2020 Charity Parkerson
Editor: BZ Hercules & Consultants
Photographer: Golden Czermak with FuriousFotog
Cover model: Caylan Hughes
ISBN: 978-1-946099-79-2

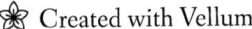

INTRODUCTION

THERE'S A DIFFERENCE BETWEEN LUCK AND
FORTUNE; THESE MEN HAVE NEITHER.

Lucky is easily the unluckiest person on the planet. Most people might say he has bad taste, but really, it's misfortune. He tries to meet nice guys. Unfortunately, he always ends up with the worst people imaginable. The only good guy Lucky knows looks wretched on paper. He owns a biker bar and runs with the roughest crowd. Lucky can't stay away.

If Damon knows two things, it's where to buy the best liquor and that Lucky is trouble. For whatever reason, Damon can't stop pulling Lucky from every fire, and Lucky starts a lot of unnecessary blazes. There's just something about him, though. Damon can't tell him no.

When Lucky pits his blind determination

against Damon's bitterness, it becomes a race to see which of them can fail the fastest. After all, there isn't an ounce of self-preservation between them. Some people are simply unfixable.

ONE

THE PIT in Lucky's gut grew with every passing moment. There had always been something missing inside him. He swore he felt the darkness turning blacker every day. Yet he kept smiling. His boyfriend, Javier, hadn't wanted to come to Tobin and Sergio's wedding with him. That was fairly par for the course with Javier. He never wanted to do anything Lucky wanted to do. Javier found Lucky's life tedious and didn't consider it his responsibility. If Lucky wanted to do anything he liked, he had to do it alone. Lucky was used to that.

In this case, Tobin and Sergio weren't really Lucky's friends, per se. The pair had invited Lucky to their wedding, nonetheless. They were already married and had been for a while. But Tobin had been battling cancer, and they had chosen to wait on a wedding. Lucky liked Tobin, so he had shown. Without Javier to keep him in check, Lucky had made one poor decision after the other all night, starting with drinking too much and ending with leaving the reception with Damon.

Damon owned a bar Lucky frequented. He was the only person on the planet who had stuck by Lucky's side without also expecting sex in exchange for tolerating him. Not that Lucky would turn down sex with Damon, but he had known Damon would be a safe friend to hang out with for the night. The guy was way too jaded to want Lucky. Plus, he not only thought Lucky was much too young for him, he also saw Lucky for his true self. Damon knew Lucky was a mess. Sure, Lucky modeled and played bit roles on television. People called him sexy and beautiful. Maybe he was, but Lucky had been trapped behind this face his entire life. He didn't look the same on the inside. It always took men a few months, but—without fail—they saw his true face in the end. Eventually, he made each and every one strike out against him. Lucky made people hate themselves for wanting him. Then they hated him too. That pit grew tonight. He felt it in his gut. Tonight would be the night he made Javier strike out.

The tension had been brewing for about a month now, turning uglier by the moment. He already walked on eggshells. Things would explode soon.

That knowledge didn't stop Lucky from smiling and teasing Damon nonstop. It was like there were two people inside him. One waited for the ax to drop. The other basked in the glow of triumph each time Damon laughed. Damon didn't smile often. Lucky needed to be the reason at least one person found joy. Damon was the only one who gave him that satisfaction.

Like everything in life, Lucky's time with Damon was temporary. The closer time creeped to the end of the night, the darker Lucky's mind turned. It was ridiculously hot in L.A. right now, even at night. Combining that heat with the high winds warning that was in effect, the night was a recipe for wildfires. Lucky felt the danger brewing in the air. He moved to the edge of the bluff where Damon had brought them on his Harley. They had spent hours staring at the lights twinkling across the city and talked about nothing while never being quiet. A gust of wind nearly knocked Lucky off his feet. He closed his eyes and spread his arms wide. Lucky felt weightless with the wind whipping around him—like he could fly.

"I don't know how you stand being that close to the edge. Heights are not my friend."

A smile tugged at the corners of Lucky's mouth. "Heights are harmless."

"Unless you fall." There was no missing the hard note to Damon's tone. Damon always sounded somewhat chastising when he spoke to Lucky—like Lucky was the bad kid in class who needed to constantly be kept straight. Maybe he was bad. All it would take was one step and he could fly for real. Then he wouldn't need to be kept in line any longer. Lucky would be free. His foot lifted. He debated whether he would take that irrevocable step forward or move back. His shirt tightened around his torso as Damon snagged the material and pulled him back.

"All right, No Fear. Time to go. I have to open the bar in a few hours, and I'd like to get a couple of hours of sleep before then."

A hint of disappointment ran through Lucky before he turned and set eyes on Damon. As always, Damon took his breath. It had nothing to do with his looks. Damon was a sexy guy. He was easily six-two and had shoulders for days. His light-colored red hair begged for Lucky to run his fingers through it. It looked soft, like the slight curl to each lock would glide through his fingers. None of that was what

4

drew Lucky to Damon, especially since Lucky was rarely single for long enough to go after Damon. No, it was Damon's eyes. They were blue and haunted. He was black on the inside too. Lucky could see Damon's soul through those gorgeous baby blues. Damon was broken. Just like Lucky.

Lucky pasted on a smile he didn't feel and let Damon steer him toward the Harley. He hooked his arm around Damon's waist. "I had a great time tonight. You're not always a complete stiff."

Damon snorted. "Sure I am. I've already lived my party days. This was nice, though. I haven't stayed up all night talking in years."

The admission warmed Lucky's chest. He felt oddly proud of himself—like he had done good. Lucky didn't ruin the moment by opening his mouth. Instead, he straddled the bike behind Damon and enjoyed the ride back to the historic hotel where the wedding and reception had been held. Lucky knew Damon only tolerated him. They weren't really friends. Lucky wasn't sure why Damon bothered with him at all, to be honest. He was grateful, nonetheless. If Damon hadn't spent the night keeping Lucky distracted, maybe tonight would have been the night Lucky took that step forward into nothing just to see if he could fly.

At the door of Lucky's Audi, Lucky slipped from the bike. He gave Damon a small wave while wearing his faked smile. The dread was already starting to build again. It was time to go home to Javier. Lucky made the drive to the upscale neighborhood where he lived with Javier Bisset. Javier was a highly respected heart surgeon twice Lucky's age. It was possible Lucky had a bit of a daddy issue, but there was also something irresistible about Javier. He was tall, dark-haired, and handsome. Intelligence always flashed in Javier's eyes, making people instinctively trust every confident word he spoke. He hadn't swept Lucky off his feet as much as he demanded Lucky get in his bed. Lucky had simply been too weak to say no. It was nice not having to make decisions, especially since Lucky almost always made bad choices.

The lights were still on as Lucky came through the door, as if Javier still waited for him. He barely stepped one foot inside the three-story mansion before he found himself frozen in place. His shoulders fell. Lucky's well-worn luggage set sat parked in the foyer. Javier was nowhere in sight. He moved to the toiletries bag that sat on top of the other pieces. Lucky unzipped the bag just enough to confirm his suspicions. His things were inside.

Lucky's breathing sped up. He worried he might hyperventilate as he searched the usual places where Javier spent time when he was home. The living room, kitchen, theater room, and Javier's office were empty. Lucky jogged up the stairs with his heartbeat pounding in his ears. He should take his things and go. Javier had obviously hoped Lucky would leave without argument. Lucky didn't want to fight. He wanted an explanation. It had been one wedding. One fucking night without Javier at his side. How did one time of wanting to do what he wanted to do lead to this? Lucky could be better. He could try harder.

Their bedroom door was closed, proving Javier had gone to bed without him. No doubt Javier slept peacefully with no hint of concern over ending them. Lucky opened the door with more force than intended. His fear had him turning into the inelegant guy he was inside. Lucky's breath caught in his throat. His heart stopped beating. The world seemed to darken around the edges of his vision. Javier wasn't alone. As much as he wished he hadn't seen a thing, Lucky noticed every detail. The flush on the guy's cheeks. His blond hair. Javier's annoyance over being interrupted. Lucky knew he could turn away and Javier wouldn't even miss a beat. His feet wouldn't budge.

With an aggravated growl, Javier crawled from the bed and grabbed his robe. He was still hard. Lucky's presence hadn't affected him in any way other than being an unwanted frustration.

Lucky automatically moved to the hall as Javier headed his way. Javier closed the door behind him and pinned Lucky in place with his stare. "Did you not see your bags in the foyer?"

"I saw them." Lucky sounded so damn calm, even he didn't know how he managed it.

Javier motioned for Lucky to get moving, as if that was all that needed to be said.

Even though Lucky knew he would hate himself afterward, because Lucky always hated himself, Lucky heard himself begging for more explanation. "Are you seriously done with me just like that? I go to one wedding without you and there's already someone else in our bed."

"My bed," Javier corrected. He took an audible breath, as if tired by Lucky's presence. "You're just candy, Lucky. You knew that going in. You're very pretty to look at, but that's it. Everyone is sleeping with someone else on the side. After all, that's where you were tonight, right?"

Lucky swallowed the hurt. No way would he look even more pathetic by saying he hadn't been with someone else. "Sure." Javier was right. Everyone cheated. Just because he never had didn't mean anything. Maybe one day he would. After all, everyone always cheated on him. It might be his turn someday.

Javier smiled as if satisfied their conversation was at an end. "See? No hard feelings. You knew this was temporary."

"Of course." What else could Lucky say? He hadn't thought they were permanent. No one ever was. He had known this was coming. "Have a nice life, Javier."

"You too, Lucky."

Like that, Lucky jogged back down the stairs and grabbed his things. He had gotten exceptionally good at moving his four bags from place to place over the years. Tonight was no different. He never had anywhere to go. Lucky was a little worse off this time since he had next to no money left to his name. He wasn't flat broke, but he couldn't afford to get a place to live. Lucky had enough to hit the closest liquor store and get plastered beyond consciousness. He should have taken that final step tonight. It wasn't too late.

THE HOUSE FELT EMPTY. TO BE HONEST, Damon's house always felt devoid of life. The nights were the worst, though. It had been almost nine years since Damon's son Mack had committed suicide, leaving Damon to pace the floor at night. He had long past accepted that there was nothing he could have done. Mack had been schizophrenic. He had gotten incredibly good at hiding his symptoms. In fact, Damon had believed his son was in the best place in his life before he caught Mack beating up his boyfriend in their driveway. That boyfriend had been Tobin. The same Tobin that Damon had watched marry tonight. Two days after the driveway incident, Mack had leapt from a bridge in a town four hours away. He hadn't wanted Damon to clean up the mess. Damon thought about that a lot, wondering if that was why Mack had hidden how bad things had become. Had he not wanted Damon cleaning up his mess? Damon didn't know if it would be better or worse to know. He would have done anything, gone to any extreme to save his son. Now it was too late. All he could do was pace the floor alone now with no real answers.

Tonight, life had been a little better. He hadn't

felt quite so alone in the world, which was weird considering he had been with Lucky. Damon spent a lot of time with other people. He owned a bar that was always busy. There were plenty of people around if he wanted to chat. Yet it had been Lucky Whitehall who had made him smile. Jesus. Lucky was a goddamn mess. Damon wasn't sure exactly how old Lucky was, but Damon imagined he had at least fifteen years on the guy. There wasn't a gay man alive who hadn't drooled over Lucky. He was probably around five ten, and that was literally the only average thing about Lucky. His inky black hair always hung in his light gray eyes, tempting a person to swipe it away so they could get a better look. Every inch of Lucky had been sculpted to tempt others. He had dimples and perfect teeth. The guy smiled all the goddamn time, even though nothing ever went right for him. He was too damn much of everything. Oddly, nothing about Lucky's appearance was what enticed Damon. There was something else about Lucky—something Damon couldn't articulate—that made the guy like a siren's call. Damon wanted to shake Lucky and force him to be real with Damon for five goddamn minutes. He wanted Lucky to just fucking say what he wanted from Damon. Damon needed to know why Lucky kept seeking him out so he could shut the guy down or shrug it off. As things stood now, Lucky baffled the fuck out of Damon and Damon hated that. The guy took up too much of Damon's headspace. Damon needed to cut him out.

The cellphone Damon left on the coffee table rang. Damon checked the face. It was his alarm company. He quickly pressed the phone to his ear.

"Hello?"

"Damon Patterson?"

Damon's forehead furrowed in his impatience. "Yes?"

"This is Sonya with Steel Security. The alarm at one zero four Stanton Place has been activated. Can you confirm?"

Damon pinched the spot between his eyes where a pain bloomed. "I'm not on site currently, so I didn't set it off."

"We'll dispatch the police."

Damon blew out a breath. "Okay. I'm heading that way."

"Would you like the officer who responds to call and let you know what they find?"

Even though the woman couldn't see him, Damon nodded. "Please. I'll still head that way in case anything needs to be boarded up or whatever, but yeah. I'd like to know what's going on."

After making arrangements to have the responding officer call his cellphone, Damon quickly threw on a t-shirt. He took his truck since he didn't relish riding across town on his Harley in his pajama pants. Halfway to the bar, his cellphone rang. Damon hit the button on his steering wheel to answer the call from handsfree.

"Hello?"

"This is Officer Hollis with the LAPD. Am I speaking with Damon Patterson?"

"Yes."

"Mr. Patterson, I'm at the Road Clan. Your alarm representative passed along your number. There was a guy waiting outside when we got here. He has a key and claims you've given him permission to stay in the upstairs apartment, but—for whatever reason—his alarm code isn't working."

If Damon hadn't been driving, he would have beaten his head on the steering wheel. "Is his name Lucky?"

"Yes, sir."

Damon took a steadying breath. "It's fine. I'm sorry you had to make the trip out. Lucky has permission to be there. I recently changed the alarm code and didn't think to give it to him. I'll disarm the alarm from my phone and he's welcome to stay. Thanks again for checking it out."

"Yes, sir, Mr. Patterson. Have a good night."

"You too." Damon disconnected the call and then dug out his phone. The first red light he came to, Damon quickly disarmed the alarm. He was almost at the bar and he was too irritated to turn around. At least, that was what he told himself. There was only one reason Lucky would be looking for a place to crash. He had burned through another man. The last time Lucky had come to him, needing to use the apartment above the bar, some dude had beaten the shit out of him. Rage boiled in Damon's gut. So help him, if he got there and there was a single bruise on Lucky's skin, Damon would kill someone. He wanted to think his outrage had to do with Lucky being with him all night. If Lucky got his ass kicked, it would be Damon's fault. Damon knew the truth, though. Nobody put their goddamn hands on Lucky and got to keep them.

When he turned in the parking lot, the patrol car was headed out and Lucky was still carrying his suitcases inside. Even from inside his truck, he saw how defeated Lucky looked. He had his head down and his shoulders were rolled forward, as if they held the weight of the world. Lucky glanced behind him when Damon closed his truck door. For a moment, Damon swore Lucky's shoulders dipped even lower before he visibly straightened. He waited for Damon to reach the stairs.

"Is that your only bags or are there more in the car?"

"This is it."

Damon eyed the luggage. Lucky had two bags strapped together to make them easier to carry in one hand. In the other, he had another suitcase and there was a duffle bag hanging from his shoulder. With a nod, Damon jogged up the stairs and relieved Lucky of the two bags that were strapped together. Together, they headed into the apartment. The place had been mostly empty since Tobin moved in with Sergio. Lucky had stayed there for a few weeks several months back. That was it. To Damon, the apartment was the place he had given to his son's only love. He didn't know if he could handle anyone else moving in. Damon didn't know why he hadn't hesitated to offer the place to Lucky, especially since he wasn't sure he even liked Lucky sometimes. Lucky always turned up when he was in trouble— like a bad penny. Maybe Damon just had a soft spot for bad things. After all, most people had considered his son a lost cause.

Neither of them spoke until they were inside. "I'm sorry." Lucky didn't look Damon's way as he made the apology.

"Don't be. If you had called first, I would have given you the new alarm code."

With his gaze locked on his hands, Lucky nodded as he unnecessarily rearranged his bags. "I didn't want to wake you." He flashed Damon an unnatural smile. It looked strained as hell. "I suppose this was worse."

Damon brushed the claim aside. "Do you want to tell me what happened?"

Lucky lifted one shoulder in an uncomfortable-looking shrug. "Not really."

This was another example of why Damon always wanted to shake the shit out of Lucky. "Did I get you in trouble?"

"I'm a grown man. You can't get me in trouble."

Damon bit back a growl. "You know what I mean."

Lucky shook his head. "This has nothing to do with you. Thank you for being my friend."

Fuck. That was how Lucky did it. He would go from fake as hell to blindly vulnerable in a heartbeat.

Damon found himself shifting from foot to foot. "I guess I should let you settle in. Don't bankrupt me by drinking the bar dry."

A bright smile exploded across Lucky's face. "You know me well."

He really didn't. Damon wasn't sure anyone knew Lucky at all. "See you in a few hours."

Lucky nodded.

Damon turned away before he did something stupid—like offer any more help. He couldn't fix Lucky and it wasn't his job. Damon just wished he didn't feel so much like it was.

TWO

AS MUCH AS Lucky had wanted to drink Damon's bar dry, he hadn't. Instead, Lucky had slipped down the stairs inside the apartment that led to the bar's storeroom and grabbed a few bottles of water. After stashing them in the otherwise empty refrigerator in the apartment, Lucky had dragged his suitcases to the bedroom. For half a second, he had considered making the bed. There were linens in the closet. Instead, Lucky had fallen across the bare mattress and stared at the ceiling all night.

When the sun rose, Lucky unpacked. He kept his mind blank as he made the bed and put his toiletries in the bathroom. With everything in its place, Lucky started making a list of everything he needed—like food and toilet paper. He also needed to do a few gigs to make money, but he didn't bother writing that down. Having to scratch half the things off the list because he couldn't afford them would be all the reminder he needed. At the last second, rather than scratching anything out, Lucky simply made a quick note at the edge of the paper to figure out what he could afford as he went.

Before he could get his shoes on to head out, Damon came through the door. Lucky had no right to complain about him not knocking. It was literally Damon's place. Damon carried a four-foot-tall lamp. It looked like an old-fashioned streetlamp from a picturesque village. It was nice.

While smiling brightly and without even saying hello, Damon planted the lamp at Lucky's feet like a proud papa. "Do you know what this is?"

"It's a lamp." Even Lucky heard the confusion in his voice.

Damon held his stare. "Do you know what your problem is?"

Lucky knew this one too. "I had abusive parents. Now I seek validation from men, but—so far—they've only proven what my parents always said. That no one will ever love me, and I will spend my life alone. So I move from one unhealthy relationship to the next because I'm too dumb to get the message."

Damon blinked at Lucky's diarrhea of the mouth.

Lucky flashed him a tight smile as if he hadn't told Damon his entire life story in one breath. "I've had a lot of therapy. Obviously, it didn't work."

"No." Damon sounded hard. "That's not the issue I'm referencing. Your problem is that everything you own will fit in four bags, making it way too easy for you to move from place to place. Do you know what this is?" Damon asked again, shaking the lamp at him.

Damon made him question himself. This time when he answered, he dragged out each word, sounding unsure. "It's a lamp?"

Damon gave him a sharp nod. "It's your lamp. Wherever you end up next, don't you dare let them take your goddamn lamp from you. No way this sucker is fitting in a suitcase. This is your fucking lamp."

Lucky accepted Damon's gift. As his fingers wrapped around the base, a warmth spread through Lucky's chest. This was his lamp. He didn't know where to put it. In fact, he couldn't stop looking at it. There was an odd pressure behind his eyes. It was kind of like he wanted to cry or something. He glanced around the room, trying to decide where to put it. Finally, he decided on a spot that would have light shining over his shoulder when he sat on the couch. He plugged it in and turned the knob. It didn't do anything. A hint of disappointment hit. Damon was right. This was his lamp. It didn't work.

"It probably just needs a new bulb or something." Damon sounded uncomfortable.

Lucky did what he always did. He pretended everything was fine. He flashed Damon a smile. "It's no big deal. This place has plenty of light without it. I'll figure it out later. Thank you. I love it."

Damon wiped his hands on his jeans and gave Lucky a nod. "I have to get back downstairs. Deliveries and whatnot."

"Would you like some help?"

Damon glanced around, as if trying to think of a way to tell Lucky he didn't want his help. His gaze landed on the list that sat on the bar that separated the living room from the kitchen. To Lucky's horror, Damon ripped the paper from the scratchpad and put the list in his pocket. "I'll pick these things up for you later." Damon pulled his wallet from his pocket and dug out a twenty. He held the money out to Lucky. "First, I need you to run across the street to Randy's diner and grab us breakfast. They're usually pretty quick with to-go orders. Get whatever, I'm not picky. When you get back, you can fill out some paperwork so I can get you on the payroll."

Lucky didn't move. Not even to take the money. "Why are you doing this?"

Damon closed the distance between them and tucked the twenty in Lucky's pocket. "I've got shit to do, Lucky. Get moving."

With a nod, Lucky stepped around Damon and headed for the door. Damon wanted breakfast and Lucky needed to do something right for once in his goddamn life. Otherwise, he truly didn't deserve Damon's friendship.

———

IT ONLY TOOK ONE LOOK AT LUCKY TO SEE HE hadn't slept. Other than giving Lucky a job and something tangible to claim as his own, Damon didn't know how to help. He was eaten alive with curiosity. Damon wanted to know what happened last night. He already knew Lucky would never say. Last time, even though some guy had obviously beaten the hell out of him, Lucky hadn't told Damon a single detail. For reasons Damon hadn't deciphered, Lucky kept everything inside. Damon had to let it be that way or risk Lucky would stop reaching out for help. That was one outcome Damon couldn't live with. He had already failed one boy in need.

With Lucky getting their breakfast, Damon pulled the list Lucky had written from his pocket. It was the most heartbreaking collection of items Damon had ever seen. Lucky was literally starting with nothing but his clothes. Then there was the tiny notation about not having the money for everything. Damon couldn't let this go on. If Lucky needed help, Damon couldn't turn a blind eye.

He quickly took a picture of the list and attached it to a text to Frost, asking him to pick up everything and deliver it to the apartment. Frost wasn't his first choice. He would have preferred to ask Tobin, but Tobin was in the Bahamas on his overdue honeymoon. While Damon knew a lot of people, he didn't know many who would do this. Honestly, he didn't know if Frost would.

Frost: *I have questions.*

Damon: *Just helping someone down on their luck. Let me know the total and I'll send you the funds.*

Frost: *What else will you give me?*

Damon swallowed a sigh. Honestly, he was a little tired of everyone. Damon was the guy who always stopped his life for everyone else. Yet the moment he needed any help from anyone else, it became a favor. He was tired and Frost had picked the right day.

Damon: *On second thought, never mind. I've got a new guy starting today. He can handle the morning bullshit around here while I do this myself.*

Frost: *I was only playing, sexy. I don't mind grabbing everything.*

Damon: *It's cool. I've got it.*

Frost: *That's fine. Ten bucks says it's for your problem child, Lucky. I don't care to run errands for the pretty boy.*

Since Damon was already aggravated, he didn't bother responding. Frost could go fuck himself. Damon was getting a little tired of him anyhow. Lucky used his back to push open the door to the bar as he carried in their food. He had a plastic bag draped over his arm and a drink in each hand. Damon rushed to help him.

He took a coffee and the bag. "It smells good."

Lucky flashed him a smile as he headed toward a table. "Yeah. They were having a two for twelve ninety-nine meat lover's biscuit combos. One of us might end up having a heart attack afterward, but they look delicious."

Without thought, Damon pulled a chair out for Lucky to sit. He played off the move by acting like nothing happened. "I've had the meat lover's biscuit and you're right."

Lucky laughed. The muscles in Damon's stomach tightened inexplicably. Lucky didn't give him time to puzzle over it. "About which part? The deliciousness or the heart attack?"

With a chuckle, Damon planted his ass in the seat across from Lucky. "Both." He helped Lucky unpack the food. The whiff of grease and regret slapped Damon in the face. It was two of his favorite scents.

While they ate, Lucky kept him entertained. He told stories about people he met at random, because —apparently- everyone just talked to him everywhere he went. Damon made two discoveries. One, he knew that. He hadn't realized it before, but everyone did talk to Lucky. At the reception, Damon had watched almost everyone Lucky passed stop him to chat. The second discovery wasn't as enlightening or as comfortable. Damon liked spending time with Lucky. The guy was genuinely nice and funny. He actively listened when other people spoke. That last bit probably fed Damon's first realization. Lucky cared what other people had to say. Therefore, everyone told him everything. Lucky's natural charm made breakfast fly.

Damon checked his watch as he popped the last bite of biscuit in his mouth. "How much do you know about bartending?" Damon asked around his food.

"I know how to read the labels and pour."

Damon nodded and pushed away from the table. "Good. You'll be alone this morning for a few hours. I have some errands to run." He didn't slow and let Lucky argue. "The place doesn't officially open for another two hours, so you can spend that time making sure the guys stocked the beer fridge behind the bar before they left last night. If not, please do that. The beer is in the storeroom. Also, kind of walk around for a visual check to ensure they cleaned. You should be fine after opening. There are only a few regulars who pop in before noon. They're usually just bored or alcoholics. Nothing you can't handle."

"Okay." Lucky truly looked like he would be fine.

Damon didn't understand why he trusted Lucky so much, but he did. Unfortunately, he kept thinking of a million things a new hire should do and know. "Oh, yeah. We'll fill out your paperwork later. I can't afford to pay you much, but I'll pay you daily. Plus, all the guys tip. The price list is taped to the counter next to the register. Just type the price in and the register does the rest. What else?"

Lucky laughed and pushed him toward the door. "I know your number, sweetie. Just go. I'll be fine. You'd be amazed how good I am at winging it."

After Damon opened the door, he had another thought and turned. His mouth opened.

Lucky smiled.

Damon's thoughts scattered. He made a third realization about Lucky. As long as they had known each other, he hadn't seen Lucky smile for real before now. There was no twinkling charm. Damon had no desire to smile in return because such a beautiful man looked at him. Lucky's real smile was sweet and hopeful. It made Damon want to protect him. Kiss him. Feel too much. Goddamn. Damon was a blind idiot. He wanted Lucky. Probably always had. Damon had no idea where to go from here.

THE MORNING MOVED FASTER THAN LUCKY expected. The guys hadn't restocked the fridge and that kept Lucky's hands busy. Then he found the bathrooms were only halfway clean—like he was certain someone had made the attempt, but they needed more help. By the time he pulled the chain on the neon "open" sign, he had already broken a sweat. It felt good to be moving. In fact, he didn't think he would need to hit the gym today if he kept finding work to do. Lucky busied himself way more than necessary because Damon obviously trusted him way more than Lucky deserved. He had left Lucky alone to open his bar.

One time, a while back, Damon had left Lucky to sign for a beer delivery. That morning didn't count. It had been an extreme emergency and Lucky knew it had eaten Damon alive to do it. Back then, Damon had likely expected he would come back to find his bar burned to the ground. After all, Damon had been putting out Lucky's fires for a while now. That thought punched Lucky in the gut. Damon was still cleaning up the mess that was Lucky's life. Maybe, one of these days, Lucky would surprise Damon and do something good. Right now, he would start with being the best employee Damon had.

The door opened and a guy who resembled a hairy bear walked in. He was more tattoo than skin. Brown hair covered his head and half his face. Lucky imagined it probably coated his chest as well. Even though Lucky recognized him by face, no name came to mind. He was a regular at Road Clan, but they had never spoken. He smiled when he caught sight of Lucky behind the bar. He had a great smile. It was sweet—like someone could climb into the guy's lap and get read a bedtime story.

"Hey, there. Where's Damon this morning?"

"He had a few errands to run. What can I get you?"

The guy settled onto a barstool before he answered. "Miller."

Damon eyed the counter. They had things on tap and in the fridge. There was a possibility he wouldn't be that great at this. "Glass or bottle?"

"Glass. Your name is Lucky, right?"

Lucky nodded as he filled the glass.

The guy kept talking. "I've seen you in a few television shows. I'm Zeppelin. Everyone calls me Zep."

Of course he was. "You look like a Zeppelin." Lucky set the drink on the bar. "What do you do for a living, Zep?"

"I'm a doula."

Lucky blinked. Of all the things in the world he expected Zep to do, delivering babies didn't even rank. "That's amazing. Do you enjoy it?"

Zep beamed. "I love it. Of course, I've always loved babies and new life is miraculous."

Lucky found himself leaning his elbows on the bar and hanging on every word Zep spoke. He was soft-spoken and animated. Lucky completely understood why a woman would choose him to bring their baby into the world. Zep was intelligent as hell and Lucky lost track of time listening to him talk. He was so engrossed in Zep's stories that he startled when Damon materialized behind him, having slipped inside the bar from the storeroom.

Lucky tried to hide the way his hands shook from being sneaked up on from behind. He had a bit of PTSD from his childhood... and his adulthood.

Damon set his hand on Lucky's shoulder and massaged. He kept his gaze locked on Zep. "Hey there, Zep. Are you having a good day so far?"

Zep never stopped smiling. "Yep. I was just telling Lucky that I delivered two babies last night."

"You're amazing." Damon finally focused on Lucky. His blue gaze stirred butterflies in Lucky's gut unexpectedly. Lucky didn't know if it was still his bad nerves or something more. "Run upstairs and put away the things I bought, please."

Without thought, Lucky headed for the stairs inside the storeroom before it hit him that upstairs was the apartment. His steps faltered. Surely Damon hadn't spent the morning buying the stuff on that list. That was insane. Lucky found himself jogging up the stairs. As soon as he came through the door, he spotted bags upon bags scattered on the entire living room floor. His throat swelled as he crossed the room. He hadn't thought Damon had been serious about grabbing the stuff Lucky needed.

Lucky started unloading the bags. He found everything on his list along with things he hadn't considered but definitely needed. During one of his many passes around the bar as he carried things from the living room to the kitchen, he spotted a note on the countertop. Lucky picked up the scratchpad.

Lucky,

The apartment is $400 a month, if you'd like to stay. There's no need to pay a deposit or utilities. I know you won't destroy the place and the bar needs water and lights. You're no extra burden. While I realize that sounds cheap, you'll be living above a bar, so there's some noise involved in that. It's not like I could rent the place out to a stranger. Plus, having you there is like an extra layer of security after hours. Think about it and let me know. You can stay this first month for free until you're on your feet no matter what you decide.

—D.

Goddamn. Lucky had known Damon would let him crash for a few weeks because he always did. This was different. It was a fresh start. He didn't know how to accept. Lucky couldn't turn it down. He turned in a slow circle and inspected the tiny apartment with fresh eyes. The place was fully furnished since Tobin had married a millionaire. It came with a small TV and a comfortable brown couch. Lucky's throat swelled again. It was his place. He wasn't a guest or fucking anyone for a place to sleep. Lucky had a steady job and would pay rent. A pressure grew in his chest. It felt like pride. He could never thank Damon enough for this. All Lucky could do was be the best goddamn employee Damon ever had. Otherwise, Lucky had nothing to offer someone like Damon. Damon didn't want him sexually. In fact, Lucky didn't think Damon liked him at all, even as a friend. Lucky would have to change that last part. Everyone needed someone like Damon in their life. Lucky wanted to be the guy Damon needed in his. He could do it.

THREE

TWO MONTHS of Lucky helping out at the bar had Damon more rested than he had been in years. He had stopped coming in at the crack of dawn to clean up after nightshift and intercepting early morning deliveries. Lucky handled everything now, leaving Damon to sleep in before heading out to pick up coffee for them. Each day, when Damon showed up with a cup of Lucky's favorite brew, Lucky would turn brighter. It was almost as if he relished seeing Damon. That fucked with Damon's head more than he would admit, even under the threat of torture. Today was no different.

"Good morning, gorgeous."

"I don't think you're supposed to greet your boss that way, but I'll take it." He passed Lucky his coffee.

"Sorry I'm a little later than usual. The line at the coffee shop was around the block."

"You don't have to explain." Lucky sipped the specialty coffee. His eyes fell closed. "Mmmm. Totally worth the wait."

Damon's mouth went dry as he watched Lucky's orgasmic enjoyment of a drink. Lucky's eyes opened. He caught Damon staring. Neither of them looked away. The past two months had been hell.

Damon forced himself to move along. "If you've got all the pre-opening things under control, I have some payroll shit to do in my office."

Lucky set his coffee aside, as if determined to be all business. "Actually, there's something wrong with one of the taps. Tommy left a note that it's broken. I know nothing about any of that, so..."

Damon moved behind the bar and checked the tap with the sticky note attached. Lucky watched over his shoulder. His body heat seeped into Damon's back. Damon pulled open the steel door beneath the taps and checked the hoses. "It's just loose." He retightened the hose and turned away. Lucky was still in his space.

Lucky motioned toward the cabinetry. "Do you mind showing me what you did? In case it happens again."

Damon drew a steady breath and moved aside, making space for Lucky to stoop next to the hose. "Sure. Get down there and take a look. Tommy should've been able to do this too. It's pretty simple. If the hoses aren't tight enough, everything loses pressure."

He watched as Lucky inspected the system, figuring everything out by himself.

From his knees, Lucky turned his face up toward Damon. "That seems simple enough."

As Damon stared down the line of his body, he recognized his mistake. He liked the sight of Lucky on his knees way more than he ever wanted to admit. "Yeah. It's an easy system to keep flowing." Without thought, he helped Lucky to his feet. He held Lucky's hand for longer than necessary. His thumb brushed over Lucky's knuckles before his brain accepted what he had just done. Damon quickly stepped away. He tapped his knuckles on the bar. "Like I said, paperwork and all that. I'll be in my office."

"Sure." Lucky blocked the only way out from behind the bar.

Since Damon didn't want to move, he didn't call Lucky on it. "Is everything else going okay?"

Lucky clasped his hands together—like trying to

find something to do with them. "Yeah. It's just that I've been taking some cooking classes at night. No reason. Just bored, I guess. Anyhow, I bought of bunch of shit to make Beef Wellington. No idea if it'll turn out okay, but I'd like to give it a shot. Would you like to be my tasting victim?"

A smile tugged at Damon's lips. He could tell this was more important than Lucky let on. Likely, he didn't want anyone to call him on it if he wasn't good enough or quit, so he pretended the classes were for kicks. Damon got it. He usually handled his own aspirations the same way. "Yeah. Just let me know when."

Lucky beamed. "Tonight, if you're free."

Damon was always free. "Yep. I'll be there, or here. Whatever."

"Okay." Lucky twisted his fingers. "I'll let you get to work. Thank you for the coffee and the lesson. I look forward to tonight."

Damon didn't think he had ever seen Lucky nervous before. His unease made Damon question himself—like, was this a date? He hadn't thought it was a date until Lucky started acting all skittish and whatnot. Now Damon wondered if he'd read things wrong. Goddamn it. He wanted it to be a date.

"I'll just... be in my office."

They did a bit of foot shuffle where they tried to pass each other without touching while also trying to decide which way to go. Finally, Damon snagged Lucky's hips and physically shifted him to one side so he could pass. He didn't make eye contact. Touching was already too much. He didn't draw another full breath until he was alone in his office. Fuck his life. What had he done?

Two months. Exactly sixty-one days had passed since Lucky officially moved into the apartment above the bar. Every one of those had been hell. They were torture when Damon was around and even worse when he wasn't. Lucky had never met anyone he couldn't have, even if he never got to keep them. He didn't think he could have Damon. Not even temporarily. For the first time in his life, Lucky didn't want to screw up something wonderful. His fate always rested in the hands of someone he slept with. This one time, he didn't have an ax hanging over his head. He was in charge of his life. If he made a move on Damon, that would change. That was why Lucky had started taking cooking classes with Zep two nights a week. He didn't mind working at the bar. The job kept him busy and in shape. Like learning about fixing the tap, Lucky wanted to know everything about everything so he would have some skills to take elsewhere. He didn't want to rely on Damon forever. Lucky couldn't get tossed in the street with nothing but his clothes again. He needed his own money. It killed him inside, but his acting gigs had completely dried up. Even though he still had feelers out for modeling gigs, he couldn't give up a steady paycheck for a temporary one. Lucky had a bad feeling that part of his life was done.

He eyed his surroundings as the clock crept closer to noon and the place slowly filled. On the flip side of losing his dream career, Lucky had fallen in love with this bar and its regulars. The place was always packed this time of day, and that was without them serving food. They had a few snacks and that was it. People simply gravitated here—like drawn by a need to be closer to their chosen family. While Lucky had frequented this place before working here, he hadn't gotten to know anyone beyond Damon, and he hadn't come here on purpose. Damon had been taking out the trash when Lucky's boyfriend at the time had pushed him from a moving car. Lucky had pretty literally landed on the doorstep of Road Clan. The only reason Lucky ever returned was for Damon. Now he realized how much he had been missing by not getting to know these guys. They were a rugged group of tattooed miscreants and some of the best people he had ever met. There were a few assholes mixed in, but it was like that everywhere. Lucky was content. That was a lot better than he had been in a long time.

The door opened and the place fell silent. A slim, dark-haired, and perfectly styled dream walked in. Every eye followed the man as he headed Lucky's way. The place was quiet enough to hear a squirrel fart. Lucky could have met Kit halfway and brought the crowd's confusion to an end about why such a perfect specimen would grace this place. But Lucky enjoyed Kit's confidence. Kit was completely unruffled by the attention. In fact, Lucky got the feeling Kit relished every step in Lucky's direction. His suspicions were confirmed when Kit tucked an imaginary stray hair behind his ear only to have his oversized sweatshirt slide down his arm afterward, exposing his shoulder. He looked adorably out of place—like a babe lost in the woods. It was an act, of course. Despite Kit's tiny size and demure demeanor, he would eat all these men for breakfast.

By the time Kit finally reached Lucky, his sweet

brown eyes flashed with silent laughter. He knew Lucky knew his game. Sound burst to life again, as if everyone simultaneously decided it made sense Kit would be there for Lucky.

Lucky snorted as he circled the bar and hugged Kit. "Hey, babe. What brings you by?"

Kit hugged him back for real—like a genuine friend. "I have news I wanted to deliver in person."

Like that, Lucky's stomach balled tight with anticipation. "Really?" Hope rose in his chest.

Kit nodded. "I got hired for a threefold spread where I spend the day working through several poses for three separate magazines owned by the same company. They want couple shots and they said I could pick whoever I want to pose with me, as long as he's hot. I want you."

Lucky tried not to explode from the excitement. "Really?"

Kit's smile dimmed. "There's a catch. A few catches, actually."

Lucky's mood dampened a hair. "Such as?"

Kit pulled a face, but not too much since pulling faces wrinkled the skin. "The shoot is in San Fran, so we'd have to stay the night, and they're not comping rooms."

"That's no big deal. We could share and split the cost."

Kit didn't stop semi-wincing. "We'd also be nude. Together. And fully aroused."

Oh. It was like that.

Kit's expression cleared when Lucky didn't respond. "It's three different high-end magazines with us as the feature couple. The pay is seventy-five thousand. We split fifty-fifty."

Lucky covered his mouth. He would have a cushion. That meant he could go after Damon without fearing the worst.

"Would you like to dance?"

Kit blinked at the sudden interruption and the huge bear-like biker who was more tattoo than skin. His gaze skimmed the room, obviously noting there was no dance floor or music. Kit met Zep's stare. "Oh. Sweetie."

"I'll go sit down."

Kit patted Zep's forearm. "That's probably best." The moment they were alone again, Kit met Lucky's gaze as if nothing happened. "Anyhow, all you have to do is say yes and leave with me Saturday and the job is yours."

"Yes." Lucky answered before he thought about Damon. "If I can get off work, of course."

"Oh. Sweetie." Kit sounded exactly the way he had seconds ago with Zep.

Lucky rushed to fix it. "It won't be a problem. I'll be there. Thank you for asking me."

A sassy smile stretched Kit's lips. "Of course, angel. You know we always watch out for each other. If I have my foot in a door, I'll hold it open for you. Plus, there's no one else I can ask to be nude and aroused with me for this thing without fear of it being taken the wrong way. Now." His gaze skimmed the room again and landed on Zep. He blindly patted Lucky's arm. "I'm about to go sit on the biker daddy's lap and let him tell me a story."

Lucky bit back a smile. "Zep is a doula. He has stories."

Kit still didn't look his way. "Damn. Those make a lot of money in L.A. All the celebs and new agey peeps want to have their babies at home."

While Lucky had been busy with Kit, his replacement had come in for the day. Since Lucky usually got started around five in the morning, going behind the night shift to clean up, he was out by noon most days. For a minute, he watched Kit charming Zep. He needed to talk to Damon before Damon left for the day. They had dinner plans, but Lucky would be a nervous wreck all day if he didn't ask about this weekend now. He headed for the office.

Before Lucky stepped inside, he knocked on the open door. "Are you busy?"

Damon glanced up from his paperwork. "Not with anything that can't wait. Did Dale come in?"

Lucky nodded.

Damon motioned for him to come in. "Shut the door behind you. It's getting loud out there. I swear you being here has turned all my customers into day drinkers."

Without thought, Lucky snorted. "I get off at noon, so that theory doesn't hold water."

"Exactly. You get off at noon, so they're all waiting to ask you to lunch."

Lucky shook his head. "I've been here two months. No one has asked me to lunch yet."

Damon leaned back in his chair. A slow and sexy smile stretched his lips. "Yeah. I have a theory on that too."

Goddamn. Lucky couldn't recall the topic. He had never wanted anyone like this. Lucky had been tempted by other men. He had been desperate in the past and on the verge of homelessness. There had been plenty of times he would have gone home with anyone who could support him. This was different. It was primal. He forced himself to stay on task.

"I hate to ask, but I need this weekend off."

Damon's expression snapped closed. His tone turned business-like. "Of course. You never take time off, so it's not like I can complain." He pushed to his feet and moved to the dry-erase board that showed the monthly schedule. He grabbed a marker. "Did you need Friday too, or just Saturday?"

They were closed on Sundays, so that day wasn't an issue, but they should probably get there a day early to be rested for the shoot. Lucky sat on Damon's desk. "Yes."

While Lucky stared at the way Damon filled out his jeans, Damon erased Lucky's name from Friday and Saturday. He wrote in his own before setting the marker aside. "It's too late to ask anyone else to cover for you. I'm good to handle it. What do you have going on?"

"I got a modeling gig, but I have to go to San Francisco for the weekend for the shoot."

A bright smile lit Damon's face. He slapped Lucky's thigh and squeezed. "That's great. I know that's what you really want to be doing. I've been worried that by keeping you here, I'm killing your dreams."

Damon's hand was still on Lucky's thigh. He stood too close. Smelled too good. Lucky swallowed, trying to ignore the heat of Damon's palm. "Nah. I've still had my ear to the ground. My friend Kit got me the gig."

"That's great." He squeezed Lucky's thigh again. Lucky couldn't tear his gaze away from Damon's rugged face. He had some scruff on his jaw that Lucky knew would leave marks on Lucky's skin. Damon licked his lips, looking nervous. Between that sexy move and the hand on his thigh, Lucky could barely think. He swore he felt the tension rising in the room like a physical thing. "About tonight."

Lucky set his hand on Damon's so he wouldn't pull away. "What about it? Are you trying to back out?"

Damon dropped his gaze to where Lucky covered his hand. "No. I was just wondering..."

Lucky eased Damon's hand higher, slowly guiding Damon closer to where he really wanted Damon to touch him. "What were you wondering?"

Damon's lips parted on a breath and his gaze hooded as Lucky guided his hand even higher. A flush touched his cheeks. Being a ginger gave everything away. He wanted Lucky too. Damon's gaze lifted and collided with Lucky's. For a moment, the universe seemed to hold its breath.

Lucky pushed them over the edge. "Touch me."

Damon exploded.

Lucky found himself hauled to his feet. Damon's tongue invaded his mouth. Lucky held Damon's shirt in a tight grip while Damon kneaded Lucky's cock through his jeans. Air refused to inflate Lucky's lungs. He had zero doubt that he was about to blow in his jeans. Not only had he never known lust like this, but Damon had no mercy. He would make Lucky walk out of his office with cum coating the inside of his underwear. Then Lucky remembered he had two hands too. He went to work on Damon's jeans. Damon sucked Lucky's bottom lip so hard that Lucky gasped. In a flash, Lucky found his face smashed against the wall and his ass bare.

Damon bit his neck before moving to his earlobe. "You can say no."

Even though Lucky realized too late how far out of his depth he was, he wasn't backing down. He wanted this. "Not happening."

A wicked-sounding chuckle caressed his ears.

Lucky lost himself in the sound.

In a heartbeat, his hips were dragged backward, and Damon was buried inside him. The condom wrapper on the floor between his feet proved Damon had more sense than Lucky did. Lucky was in such a haze of lust that he didn't comprehend a thing beyond the desire. All he could do was cling to the wall while Damon pounded inside him. Damon kept him at the perfect angle. Lucky tugged blindly at his cock, mindless to anything but the need for release. He had never been with anyone like this. It was almost violent. Primal. They were lust in its basest form. Lucky stroked and pumped, racing toward the edge.

Damon suddenly dragged Lucky back into his arms. He held Lucky tightly against his chest. His ragged breaths brushed Lucky's ear with each thrust. "You're everything I fantasized you would be."

Ecstasy rocked Lucky's soul at Damon's confession. His body shook as jets of cum landed at his feet. Damon's grip tightened as he stifled his cries against Lucky's neck. Lucky's eyes unexpectedly filled with tears. He prayed he hadn't ruined them. Damon was the only good part of his life. Lucky dropped his chin and kissed Damon's arm. He already knew Damon wouldn't show for their date tonight. This had been a mistake. Damon had gotten the only thing men wanted from him. Now he would boot Lucky from his life. That was the way things went. He was just a pretty face.

Damon snagged Lucky's chin and gently turned Lucky's face his way. He kissed Lucky so sweetly that Lucky's emotional state deteriorated even further. Even with their kiss at an odd angle, it was the most beautiful kiss he had ever experienced. It was filled with affection.

"I think you answered my question," Damon said as he pulled away.

Lucky had no idea what he meant. "What question?"

"About tonight. I think it's safe to say that it's a date."

A smile exploded across Lucky's face. "Yeah. It's a date."

His smile melted away as Damon's cock slipped from his ass. Damon turned Lucky in his arms and claimed a proper kiss. Lucky clung to Damon's chest and savored every stroke of Damon's tongue. This had been earth-shattering. Lucky wouldn't forget this. Even when Damon stood him up later, Lucky would cling to the memory of the way Damon kissed him now. Damon's kiss felt like the closest to love Lucky had ever been. It would have to be enough.

FOUR

IF DAMON KNEW NOTHING ELSE, he knew he had to have more of Lucky. Damon's body hummed the entire day. He had sex. Damon wasn't a monk. He had a fuck buddy who worked out of town. They got together whenever Frost was home. It was just a way to scratch a mutual itch or whatever. This was different. Terrifyingly different. Damon's hands shook like he had spent the morning doing coke and couldn't wait for his next high. There were so many issues with the way he felt. Damon didn't know where to start.

He had purposely never touched Lucky before now. Damon had known there would be no going back if he did. He didn't know what happened today.

His hand had landed on Lucky's knee. That was it. That was the exact moment Damon had gone too far. When Lucky had covered his hand, Damon had been incapable of pulling away. Then Lucky had begun the slow guide toward his cock. Fuck. Damon went hard again just thinking about it.

Lucky had so much confidence in his ability to seduce that he was impossible to resist. Damon would like to think he was old enough to know better and control himself. Nope. He was a lost cause when it came to Lucky. Damon had been secretly wanting him for too long. That was the gist of things. For almost two years, Damon had been helping Lucky through one horrible decision right after the other. He told himself he had to help save who he could. That wasn't the truth, though. The truth was that Damon had been taking the trash out one night and the most beautiful man he had ever set eyes upon literally landed at his feet. He looked like a fallen angel. Instead, he had been pushed from a moving car by one in a long stream of abusive boyfriends. It hadn't mattered how Lucky had ended up there. Damon felt like Lucky had been literally gifted to him. They were so different in every way—age and character—that Damon fought against himself. The truth had always been unavoidable. Damon wanted to be Lucky's man.

After a long afternoon of overthinking his entire life's choices, Damon ended up being ten minutes late to Lucky's. He knew immediately that had been a serious misstep. The brittle edge that had disappeared from Lucky's features in the last two months was back. Damon's stomach dropped the second Lucky answered the door. Lucky's smile was fake as hell, making Damon twice as bright—something he was definitely not.

"I don't smell anything cooking."

Lucky's expression turned guilty. "I didn't think you'd show."

That was all it took to kill Damon's discomfort. His brow furrowed. Damon's features hardened with zero input from his brain. "Why in the hell wouldn't I show?"

Lucky shifted from foot to foot, looking like a squirming child. Damon found himself eyeing Lucky from head to toe. He wore baggy jeans and no shoes. His bottom lip was swollen—like he had almost chewed it raw, worrying at it.

Damon's ire disappeared. Lucky didn't know how to be with anyone who didn't mistreat him. Damon couldn't stand the idea of Lucky being scared of him. He closed the distance between them and claimed Lucky's lips. Damon felt the tension drain from Lucky as he kissed Damon back. He stroked Lucky's jaw, still trying to soothe him. Damon poured his heart into their kiss, trying to will Lucky into understanding how much he cared. Maybe Damon had a lot going on in his head. Not only was he a lot older than Lucky, Lucky worked for him and was Damon's tenant. On top of all that, Lucky had a lot of issues and Damon couldn't fix him. This was a huge mistake. Damon didn't want to stop making it now. They both deserved some happiness.

Damon lightly brushed his lips across Lucky's and stroked Lucky's cheek with his knuckles. "I'm sorry I'm late. Would you like me to take you to dinner?"

Lucky's eyes were glazed over, as if still lost in their kiss. "The guys downstairs will see us leave together."

Damon shrugged. "They saw me come up here. Plus, everyone already knows we're friends."

"Am I ruining your life?" Lucky worked on looking panicked again. "Before today, I had a lot of thoughts about how I was risking everything by wanting you. But I didn't think about how you might look to everyone else, and I don't want to embarrass you."

Something about knowing that Lucky had been worrying about wanting him brought out Damon's possessive side. "I don't give a fuck what anyone thinks. There's not a goddamn thing wrong with me recognizing a good man when I see one and taking my shot. Now, I'm on my Harley, so if we're going, I have to grab the extra helmet from the office. Are we going?"

With his bottom lip between his teeth, Lucky visibly fought a grin. He nodded.

Damon kissed Lucky again, because—in the face of Lucky's surety that he would be let down again—Damon would be goddamned if he failed him. He really liked Lucky. Maybe things weren't ideal, and he had concerns, but he genuinely *liked* Lucky. He hadn't felt this way in a long time. No one would be hurting Lucky again, especially Damon. They were about to do this thing. Fallout be damned.

LUCKY DIDN'T KNOW WHAT TO EXPECT FROM A date with Damon. They had known each other a couple of years, but this was different. Lucky still hadn't gotten past Damon showing up. Damon always treated Lucky like he genuinely cared and that was a mind fuck, for real. He had spent the day swinging wildly between being blown away by what happened in Damon's office and terrified at the idea he had ruined their friendship. It honestly hadn't crossed his mind he should bother cooking. Lucky had been one thousand percent certain Damon wouldn't show. He hadn't been mentally prepared for this date.

As the night unfolded, Lucky slowly came to the realization there was no way he could have readied himself for a proper night out with Damon. First, Damon took them for a ride along the coast before stopping at an outdoor bar and grill. The place had smokers going and grills crackling. The scent of cooking meats floated from every direction. Round patio tables with bright umbrellas and flickering candles littered the area around the wooden shack. Lucky's stomach growled as he climbed from the back of Damon's Harley. This place was nothing like his usual dates. Men always took Lucky to five-star restaurants where they lectured him on healthy eating and berated every item he ordered. After all, as Javier had pointed out the day that he dumped

Lucky, Lucky was only a pretty face. Arm candy didn't get fat.

"I'm guessing this place doesn't serve salad."

The look of horror Damon shot him was almost comical. "Do you want me to take you to a place that serves salad?"

Lucky couldn't stop smiling. "No. I was just pointing out the obvious."

Damon's shoulders relaxed, obviously relieved he would not be forced to eat rabbit food tonight. "You haven't lived until you've eaten Hugo's ribs and curly fries."

Lucky's stomach growled again, making him thankful for the loud atmosphere. "I can't remember the last time I ate a potato in any form. Much less a fry."

The way Damon's expression stayed blank said a lot. He really didn't want Lucky to know his thoughts. Damon led him to an empty table nearby. As Lucky sat, Damon pulled his chair closer, so their elbows brushed once Damon was seated. "While I applaud your discipline, there'll be none of that tonight. Tonight is an all you can eat and get fat night."

"I have a photo shoot this weekend." Lucky

hated to remind Damon of that fact since he seemed so excited to feed Lucky.

Damon flashed Lucky a wicked-looking smile. "Then I guess I'll just have to help you work off all the calories before then."

Butterflies stirred in Lucky's stomach. He was terrified of how happy Damon made him. No one was good to him for free. Before he made an idiot of himself, and said as much, two heavy beer mugs filled with ice water clunked down on the table.

"What can I get you two to drink?"

"I'm good with the water." Damon looked Lucky's way. "Do you want a beer?"

Lucky shook his head. "I'm good with the water too." After all, he was about to eat a fuck ton of carbs, apparently. The last thing he needed was to drink more calories.

The waiter nodded. "Are you two ready to order or should I give you a few minutes?"

Damon looked his way again. "What do you say? Are we doing the all you can eat thing?" There was something in Damon's eyes—like he silently dared Lucky to be bad with him.

"Yep. Let's do it."

They shared a smile. A happy sigh rang through

Lucky's mind. He hadn't known life could be like this.

The night seemed to fly as they ate and talked. Damon kept massaging Lucky's thigh beneath the table. Lucky was aware of each and every time they touched. They had already had sex. There was no need for Damon to seduce him. That was how it felt, though. Lucky felt like Damon worked to ensnare him. Damon was hypnotizing him with his secret touches.

"I know you have the photo thing this weekend, but have you still been going to auditions? You're a godsend at the bar, but I know you have dreams too."

Lucky shrugged. "I'm taking a break from all that."

Damon's eyebrows rose. "You're not giving up, are you?"

"No." Even as the denial fell from his lips, Lucky wondered if he lied. "Unless I want to do porn, and I decidedly do not want to do porn, it's kind of exhausting trying to get roles." Talking about porn had a hint of horror rising inside him. Some might say what he had agreed to do this weekend was damn near porn. If Damon was the one who planned to take nude pics with another guy this weekend, Lucky might rip off his dick, which was weird. He didn't think he had ever been jealous before. Another thought hit. What if Damon was the jealous type? Lucky wasn't a small guy, but Damon was huge. He didn't want to see Damon in a rage. Lucky found himself practically squirming in his seat.

"About my photo shoot this weekend. I should warn you. It's... um, a bit erotic."

Damon smiled. "Oh, really? You have my attention."

Lucky wiped his sweating palms on his jeans and licked his lips. "I wasn't expecting what happened this afternoon to happen and I'm super happy it did, but I don't want to hide anything."

"So you're taking your clothes off for pictures. That's no big deal. It's just a job."

Lucky bit his bottom lip for a second before delving deeper. "Um. Also, I won't be alone in these pictures." Lucky winced as the admission fell.

Damon slowly nodded. He wiped his fingers on his napkin. "I mean. It is just pictures, right?"

Lucky rushed to reassure Damon. "Of course. Kit is my friend and there's no sexual attraction there at all. We just have to pose together. It's not actually sexual."

For a moment, Damon stared at him in silence. Lucky saw the moment Damon chose to wade even deeper. "So what I'm hearing is: we're officially dating—like exclusively—and you don't want me to misinterpret your job as cheating. Is that right?"

The air seemed to thicken and turn muggy, making sweat break out on Lucky's skin. Until Damon said the words aloud, Lucky didn't realize how assuming he had sounded. He immediately retreated and tried blowing off the conversation. "Sorry. When you put it that way, I guess I came off as ridiculous. This is one date. Of course, I don't expect—"

Damon kissed him, cutting off Lucky's insecurities before they completely humiliated him. It was a sweet kiss. A light brushing of lips across lips. Just enough to silence Lucky's rambling.

"I appreciate you telling me," Damon said, sounding patient. "Even though I know you do the whole modeling thing, if I had seen those pictures without context, I might have gotten the wrong idea and thought you cheated. Now I know I shouldn't get jealous. See? We'll be great at this exclusive thing. Look at us, already talking about things like rational adults. We're already kicking ass at being a couple. We should enter a competition or something."

Lucky stared at Damon, completely awestruck. "What should we conquer next?"

Damon's mouth lifted in one corner in the world's sexiest smirk. "You should come home with me. We haven't tried sleeping in the same bed."

"Is that a hill we have to climb?" Lucky asked, genuinely enjoying himself.

Looking serious, Damon nodded. "Definitely. I've slept alone forever, so I'm probably a selfish sleeper. It's likely I snore, steal covers, and kick."

Lucky couldn't stop smiling. He loved being with Damon. Always had. "If that's the case, I have the cure."

"You do?" With his eyebrows raised, Damon openly pretended to wait with bated breath for Lucky's response.

He knew Damon thought he would say something about sex—like claim they just wouldn't sleep. That was exactly why Lucky didn't. "Yeah. I'll make you sleep on the couch."

Damon's eyes swam with laughter. "Damn. In my own house. That's cold."

Lucky shrugged. "Maybe I'm the one who snores and kicks. After all, no one keeps me for long. That could actually explain a lot." Lucky chuckled at the idea.

The laughter bled from Damon's expression. He turned serious in an instant. "I own ear plugs and I sleep like the dead. You can't run me off that easily. I'm not one of the weak-ass rich guys you've been with in the past."

At Damon's obvious irritation, Lucky retreated. "I'm sorry."

Damon blinked. A line appeared between his eyebrows. "Why are you apologizing?"

Lucky found himself fiddling with his napkin and then his water glass, incapable of being still. "I thought we were teasing. I didn't mean to make you mad. We don't have to spend the night together yet." His shoulders fell. He didn't know how to backpedal and make Damon smile again. Lucky always fucked up everything he touched. It was no wonder men treated him like shit. He was pretty fucking useless. The more his thoughts churned, the shallower his breathing became until Lucky balanced on the edge of hyperventilating. Damon probably wouldn't talk to him again after tonight. Lucky wished he were better at staying silent and sticking to looking pretty. He really, really hated himself. If Damon still talked to him tomorrow, Lucky would try harder. Everything started to darken around the edges.

Damon rubbed his back and kissed his temple,

making soothing sounds against his skin. Lucky took a deep breath and then another. His heartbeat slowed. "That's it, angel. Just breathe," Damon said between kisses. "I shouldn't have shown my jealous streak. You didn't deserve that. I'm sorry." Damon's hand smoothed down Lucky's arm. He urged Lucky to his feet. "Come on, baby. Let's head home."

Lucky wanted to cry. Damon amazed him, and Lucky had ruined their date. "I'll pay for dinner."

"I already paid. Not that I would have let you pay anyhow."

Confusion had the last of Lucky's brain fog clearing away. He hadn't seen Damon pay. It seemed he had been closer to a full-on panic attack than he realized. Great. No doubt this would go down in Damon's record books as the worst date he ever experienced. Lucky should go home now. The chances he wouldn't make a bigger fool of himself before the end of the night were slim to none. He always ruined everything.

THE THING WAS—IN THEORY—DAMON THOUGHT he understood what he got into by choosing to date Lucky. He knew about bits and pieces of Lucky's past. Damon knew Lucky was a mess on the inside. Until he had shown a hint of temper to Lucky, Damon hadn't realized he didn't know shit. Lucky needed a soft hand. Probably for the rest of his life. The guy had a twenty-eight-year head start before Damon showed up to fix things. Damon got the feeling Lucky had experienced way more abuse than he admitted to anyone. This was the point where most people would run. Damon couldn't.

They were halfway to Damon's house before he felt Lucky relax. His hold on Damon's waist turned loving instead of rigid. By the time they parked in Damon's garage, Damon could practically feel Lucky's exhaustion. Being terrified was draining as hell. Damon got it. He had spent all his son's teenage years frozen in fear and tired. Damon had expected the worst every single day until it happened. The grief wasn't less, but Damon had been unsurprised by Mack's suicide. No one understood that unless they had been there.

Lucky slipped from the bike and waited silently for Damon. Damon wanted the smiling boy from dinner back. He didn't know how to snap Lucky out of his inner battle. So Damon didn't try. He simply acted like nothing happened. Damon took Lucky's hand and held it as they headed inside his house.

The four bedroom and three bath home likely didn't seem like much to Lucky, but Damon was proud of it. He had worked hard and built the place mostly by himself. Obviously, he had a contractor helping him, but Damon had gotten in there and helped lift walls, tile bathrooms, and install hardwood. The place had sliding barn doors, jacuzzi tubs, and marble counters. It was his dream home, especially since it sat on sixty-four acres on the edge of Angeles National Forest. He had the quiet he craved.

Damon watched as Lucky trailed from room to room, taking the tour. Each room was pretty self-explanatory until Lucky reached Mack's bedroom. Even though Mack had been gone nine years now, it still looked like a teenager's room. Damon had stripped the bed, but Mack's clothes still hung in the closet. His posters still littered the walls.

Before Damon could explain, Lucky turned away and propped his shoulder against the doorframe. "Your son's room."

Even though it hadn't been a question, Damon nodded.

"How—"

Damon didn't force Lucky to ask. "Suicide. He was schizophrenic. Most people can live normal lives with medicine. Mack wasn't one of them."

A sad smile touched Lucky's lips. "I was going to ask how you ended up with a son."

A smile exploded across Damon's lips before he could stop it. "Um. It's kind of a crazy and sordid tale of a teenage boy trying to change his stripes with his forty-three-year-old neighbor."

Lucky snorted out a surprised laugh. He covered his mouth, as if horrified by his reaction.

Damon kept talking, hoping to soothe Lucky's embarrassment. "To everyone's horror, I was seventeen when Mack was born. We shared custody for a while, but by the time Mack was ten, he was too much for Angie. She signed her rights over to me and I went at things alone." Damon made a helpless gesture. "Obviously, I failed."

"You tried. That's a lot more than his mother did, and it's a lot more than most can say. Some people can't be saved from themselves."

Damon found himself hooking Lucky's belt loop with his finger and drawing him closer. Lucky was beautiful. It was obvious God had been in an exceptionally good mood the day he created Lucky. He wasn't just gorgeous. Lucky was blessed. His ink-colored hair shimmered when the light hit it just right. Locks always hung in his eyes, making the light silver irises seem even lighter by comparison. He had a mouth that immediately drew the eye. Lucky turned every head he passed. None of that was why Damon couldn't stay away. He wasn't complaining about Lucky's beautiful packaging, but his looks were almost too perfect for most people to handle. He likely drove weak men to the edge of sanity with the constant jealousy. It wasn't easy to date someone who everyone else wanted to steal. Lucky's looks weren't the driving force behind Damon's attraction. Damon had been ensnared by the way Lucky made him feel. Since Mack died, Damon had felt like he was a failure at loving people. He could keep a business going and be an actual adult most days, but if he loved anyone in any capacity, he killed them. Lucky looked at Damon like Damon was his only source of air. Like, for once, Damon breathed life into someone. It was empowering.

Damon lightly brushed his lips across Lucky's. "Do you know what I want more than anything right now?" Damon whispered, hoping to entice Lucky into being bad with him.

Lucky stared at Damon's mouth. "What?"

"To eat ice cream with you while watching a movie." It was worth it to see the smile that exploded across Lucky's face.

"You're so bad for my waistline."

That was probably true, but Damon intended to be good for Lucky's mental health. Plus, he would help Lucky work off the extra calories before this weekend. Some things were more important than looking good—like being happy. Damon had designs on making Lucky happier than he had ever been. He couldn't wait to watch Lucky bloom.

FIVE

THE PHOTO SHOOT wasn't as horrible as Lucky expected. It was by no means comfortable, but they were alone with the photographer for the actual nude parts. They had been sent through makeup while the staging people set up lights and whatnot. The room had been cleared of all but the female photographer when Kit and he had disrobed.

Even though the experience hadn't been wretched, Lucky was more than a little relieved to be back at the hotel. He would be even happier when he got to go home. If he hadn't ridden with Kit to San Francisco, he would have left already.

Lucky grabbed a bottle of water from the mini fridge and moved to the chair near the bathroom where Kit worked on removing the several layers of makeup they had been painted in. "How did your date go with Zep the other night?"

"Meh," Kit said as he leaned closer to the mirror and scrubbed. "We had a nice dinner and then both immediately admitted we have zero chemistry. It's like that sometimes. How are things with your bar owner?"

Lucky froze with his water bottle halfway to his mouth. He hadn't said a word to Kit about Damon. In fact, Kit didn't know Damon existed. "How did you know that?"

Kit shrugged while still focusing on his task. "Sweetie, people like you don't work at a bar unless they're after a bigger score. No way anyone frequents that place enough for you to justify working there. That leaves the owner. Process of elimination."

A hint of something unnamed wormed its way beneath Lucky's skin. "What do you mean, people like me?" Kit made him sound like a gold-digging predator.

Kit met his gaze in the mirror. "It wasn't an insult. I'm people like you. We're survivors and dreamers. The only way either of us is holding down a nine to five is if we're in it for some bigger aspiration. We weren't born for an ordinary life. I know you feel that in your bones. So, if you're holding down a steady job, it sure as hell isn't because you've given up on achieving your goals. That's why I ask again, how are things going with the bar owner?"

Kit was right. Lucky didn't believe he was meant for a nine-to-five job, but he had been happier at Road Clan than he had been always getting his hopes crushed by Hollywood. "His name is Damon."

A smile exploded across Kit's face.

Kit's satisfaction didn't stop Lucky's mouth. "He's pretty fantastic."

Lucky's phone buzzed. As if talking about Damon conjured him, Lucky had a text from him.

Damon: *How did the photo shoot go?*

Lucky: *Blessedly quick. Now I'm stuck here, and I want to come home.*

Lucky stared at his phone while waiting for Damon's response. When one didn't come, Lucky's shoulders fell. Damon was likely busy with bar business and he would get to Lucky when he got to him. That knowledge didn't stop Lucky's disappointment.

"Was that your man?"

Lucky shoved his feelings aside. "Yeah. He was asking about the photo shoot."

Kit froze and met Lucky's gaze in the mirror again. "How much did you tell him?"

"Everything."

Kit's eyebrows rose. "Are you kidding me? Did he flip out?"

Lucky shrugged. "He thanked me for assuring him that he had no reason to be jealous and for being honest. I told you he's amazing."

"Damn." Kit sounded blown away. "I can't even imagine what that must be like."

Lucky's phone buzzed again, and Lucky dropped his gaze.

Damon: *Get a cab to take you to the airport. I'll cash app you enough money to cover it. You have a flight home in two hours. I'm sending you a text with a boarding pass right now, and I'll meet you at the airport when your plane lands at LAX.*

For a full minute, Lucky stared at his phone in shock before he found any words to text back.

Lucky: *I can't believe you did that. Thank you.*

Damon: *If my baby wants to come home, he comes home. If I can't get to you, I will find another way. You can always count on me.*

Damn. Lucky had no words. He stood and

started gathering his things. It might take him a while to get through security.

"It looks like I'm flying out tonight. Damon just sent me a boarding pass. Are you okay to drive back alone?"

Kit snorted. "Always. Two nights alone in a hotel with me was too much for him, huh?"

For a moment, Lucky warred with himself. Either he made Damon look like a jealous bastard, or he admitted to being a baby who wanted to go home. In the end, he couldn't let Kit think poorly of Damon.

"Actually, I just said I was ready to be home, because—you know—I'm missing him. He sent me a boarding pass."

Kit slowly turned and eyed Lucky while Lucky rushed to gather his things.

"This one will hurt."

Lucky glanced Kit's way. "What's that supposed to mean?"

Kit didn't back down. "Look at the way you're rushing back to be with him. All those other men you've dated, they might have hit you or cheated, but they didn't matter. This one matters and it'll hurt when he's gone."

As much as Lucky wanted to say that maybe this

one would be different, Lucky's tongue wouldn't shape that lie. All men were the same. Lucky knew it was only a matter of time before the other shoe dropped. It always did. Maybe that was exactly why Lucky needed to soak up as many of the good days as he could get. He wanted the memories.

"They've all hurt one way or another. Maybe you're right and none of them have broken me the way this one will, but I'm not missing out on the good memories by anticipating the bad."

Kit smiled. "You sounded so adult just then. Maybe you have outgrown this lifestyle."

Lucky chuckled as he crossed the room and hugged Kit. "Don't get carried away. I'm by no means responsible enough to quit modeling. Thank you for this weekend. Be careful going home." He couldn't think about any of Kit's warnings. Lucky was too happy to be headed back home to Damon. He had only been away one night, and it was one too many. Lucky's brain stumbled over that thought and a hint of terror struck. Kit was right. This would hurt when it was over, and Lucky might not survive it this time. It was too late now to walk away. Lucky was already a lost cause. Damon was the one he wanted. Impending doom or not, Lucky wouldn't back down. He wanted Damon more than he feared the pain.

That had to mean something. Lucky had to find out what.

———

With Lucky out of town, Damon hadn't slept all night from worrying. Lucky had been too far away. If anything happened to him, it would take hours for Damon to get to him. It had almost been a relief when Lucky said he wanted to come home. Damon had never gotten a plane ticket so fast in his life. He had gladly gone to LAX to wait for Lucky's arrival. When he spotted Lucky, Damon damn near jogged away the distance between them. Even he couldn't explain his excitement. He filed it away as new relationship infatuation when his heart skipped a beat as Lucky kissed him hello.

"Hi." Lucky sounded breathless and his smile was bright. "I missed you."

He was so goddamn brave. Damon didn't think Lucky got enough credit for that. There was no way Damon would ignore that courage. "I missed you too. Obviously, since I didn't waste a second when you said you wanted to come home."

"Thank you for that. You're amazing. I'll pay you back."

Damon fought an aggravated sigh. "No. I wanted you home. That's on me." He took Lucky's bag and linked fingers with Lucky before heading for the exit.

Thankfully, Lucky didn't argue. "What did you do while I was out of town?"

"Worked. No one wants to work anymore. Marco didn't show up last night, so I was short a bouncer. I had to do it. Then Angelo decided he didn't want to come in this afternoon. After Riley showed up, I thought I'd get to finally get some sleep, but then I ended up short a bar back. I had just gotten home when I texted you."

Lucky stroked his hair. "Oh, baby. I'm sorry. I'll make sure you get some sleep tonight. If anything goes wrong, I'll handle it."

At the truck, Damon opened the passenger side door for Lucky and waited until he climbed inside before responding. "Nope. I'll close the place early before I let anything ruin my night with you." He leaned inside and claimed Lucky's mouth. He kept their kiss sweet, whisking his lips back and forth across Lucky's, teasing him.

Lucky buried his fingers in Damon's hair and lovingly scratched Damon's scalp. Goosebumps smattered Damon's skin. Never in a million years had he dreamed he could be this happy with Lucky, but here they were. They were on their way to something special. Damon felt it in his gut. Damon wouldn't change a thing. In fact, he felt pretty damn blessed Lucky had looked his way. He couldn't wait to see where they went next.

SIX

SOMEHOW, Lucky had managed to hang on to Damon for three months after their first date. No one was more surprised than him. Lucky had fallen in love with the quiet life Damon offered. He never dreamed he would want to settle down permanently, but he found himself craving more and more nights of doing nothing with Damon. They didn't spend every night together since it was easier for Lucky to open the bar if he slept upstairs. But other than the nights he did his cooking classes with Zep, they were almost always together during waking hours. As Lucky padded from the bathroom, wearing nothing but a towel, he was grateful for not having to go home tonight. They would be sleeping in together tomorrow and Lucky would get to hold Damon all night. He loved these nights.

Damon glanced Lucky's way from his spot on the couch as Lucky entered the room. For a moment, he stared at Lucky in silence before patting his lap. "I saved you a seat."

Lucky didn't try to hide his smile as he crossed the room and claimed his seat. "You always save the best spot in the house for me. You're amazing."

Damon kissed Lucky's shoulder as he released the footstool and reclined one end of the couch. "I want my baby to be comfortable. Speaking of which." Damon loosened Lucky's towel until the two halves fell away, leaving Lucky exposed. "Isn't that better?"

It seemed Damon was in the mood to play. That was fine. Lucky always had what he needed. "I don't know. What if I get cold?"

Without preamble, Damon cupped Lucky's balls and stroked upward until he tugged Lucky's shaft. "You won't."

An involuntary pant burst from Lucky. He liked being petted. "Don't stop."

Damon touched his lips to the shell of Lucky's ear. "Oh, baby. We're just getting started. I'm about to beat this cock until it explodes."

Lucky's eyes fell closed.

Damon squeezed Lucky's dick and tugged.

Lucky squirmed, trying to make him go faster.

A moan caressed the ear Damon kissed. "You're killing me, moving that sexy ass against me. I know all I have to do is push down my pants and I could be inside that tight hole. This is the good kind of torment, though. I like the anticipation. When you're all soft and relaxed from just blowing your load, that's my favorite time to fuck you. That's when you'll let me do anything."

Lucky's hips moved, keeping time with Damon's strokes. He needed the release Damon promised. "I'll always let you do anything." Lucky couldn't stop the confession in his time of weakness. In that moment, it was true. Any kinky thing Damon desired, Lucky was in.

With one hand still wrapped firmly around Lucky's erection, Damon snagged Lucky's jaw with the other. His index finger pushed against Lucky's lips until Lucky opened his mouth and sucked the digit.

"That's it, Lucky. Let me feel that tongue. You have no idea how perfect your mouth feels. Not only on my dick, but every place you touch me with it. Suck. Make me fantasize."

Lucky did as told. He was nearly insane with lust. He pushed against the tug of Damon's fist, silently begging for release.

Damon licked his ear, driving Lucky's madness to an even higher level. "Fuck, baby. You've got me ready to blow just feeling this ass gyrate."

He wanted to see Damon come in his pants. Lucky worked harder at grinding against Damon's erection. Damon shifted positions, pushed Lucky's knees wide, and curled the finger Lucky had been sucking inside Lucky's ass. Lucky's muscles jerked. The orgasm he barely held at bay exploded into reality. Lucky's body shook. Damon breathed heavy against Lucky's ear while he jacked Lucky's dick faster, stealing every spasm from Lucky. Lucky's breaths burst from him in rapid succession, making him sound like he had run a marathon. With his stomach painted in cum and Damon still fingering his ass, Lucky fought to claim Damon's mouth. With the awkward angle, Lucky couldn't kiss Damon as deeply as he wanted, but he tried. Despite his soul-searing orgasm, Lucky wasn't ready to stop. He wanted Damon's dick inside him. Damon's work cellphone rang.

"No." Damon's denial sounded genuinely disheartened. As he grabbed the phone and answered, Lucky slipped from Damon's lap and quickly used his towel to wipe away the cum. He didn't bother listening to Damon's conversation. Instead, he crawled onto the couch next to Damon, popped Damon's erection from his pajama pants, and sucked.

Damon drew a sharp breath and then quickly cleared his throat, trying to cover up the sound.

Lucky chuckled around Damon's cock. He wasn't sorry. In fact, he worked hard to make Damon slip again. He wanted whoever interrupted them to know they were interfering with a good time.

Damon buried his fingers in Lucky's hair and tugged, taking Lucky's mouth the way he liked. Lucky put all his skills to work. He wanted Damon's cum filling his mouth.

"Fuck yeah. Take it all. We have to hurry. I have to go to work."

Since Damon was obviously done with his call, Lucky didn't hold back. He swallowed Damon's dick like he hadn't eaten in days. Lucky sucked and bobbed, letting his saliva drip down Damon's cock. Damon's muscles tensed. Lucky took all of him and sucked hard. Damon cried out. Lucky's scalp stung as Damon pulled his hair. He pumped Lucky's mouth full of cum.

"Goddamn. Fuck. Yes. You blow my mind. Holy shit. I want to be inside you. I'm sorry I'm ruining our night. You have no idea how much I wanted to take you to bed and rock inside you until we both fell asleep from exhaustion."

Sometimes, Damon said things that shouldn't move Lucky, but—for whatever reason—Lucky nearly cried at Damon's words. It wasn't so much what Damon said as much as how he said it. Damon sounded like a man in love. Lucky knew that was wishful thinking. That was his heart wanting more than it should. Still, in that moment, Lucky would have done anything to ensure he never lost Damon.

Lucky kissed a path up Damon's body until he reached his mouth. He kissed Damon three times in quick succession before pulling away. "What's going on at the bar?"

Damon pulled a disappointed face. "Tommy is sick—like fever and all. He needs to leave. He tried calling a bunch of people, but no one will come in for him."

"I'll go. You stay here and relax."

For a moment, Damon stared at him in silence. His expression didn't give away his thoughts. He gave Lucky a sharp nod, as if coming to a decision. "Let's go together. That way, we can get through the closing shit super-fast tonight and I can still have my chance to fall asleep inside you."

Lucky kissed Damon again. He couldn't help it. Lucky was just so goddamned happy with Damon. Every day felt like a blessing. His life had never been like this. In the past, every day felt like a chore. He actually knew happiness now, and that was all due to Damon.

"Let's do it."

Lucky shot to his feet and headed for the bedroom to dress. Anything he could do to make himself indispensable to Damon, Lucky would do it. He needed Damon to need him. Otherwise, Damon had no reason to keep him. Kit was right. Losing Damon would kill Lucky. So Lucky had to make sure it never happened. If that meant slinging drinks until two in the morning, that was what Lucky would do. Lucky needed one fucking person on the planet to love him. He prayed every day that person would be Damon.

DAMON DIDN'T HAVE A LOT OF BUSY WORK TO DO while Lucky served drinks. Mostly, he was just fucking around so he could be there with Lucky.

After two hours of chatting with customers, he decided to head to his office and see if he could get anyone to answer his calls. He wanted to take Lucky home and get inside him, as promised. Lucky worked too hard already.

Before he could make the first call, there was a light knock on Damon's open office door. He glanced up from his list of phone numbers. Zep stood in the doorway, shifting nervously from one foot to the other. Damon couldn't help but smile. Zep was such a gentle giant. A teddy bear, really. To anyone who didn't know him, he likely looked terrifying. Damon imagined elderly ladies tightened their grips on their purses when Zep was near. The guy was marshmallow on the inside.

"Hey, Zep. What can I help you with?"

Zep cast a quick glance behind him before focusing on Damon. "Is it okay if I talk to you?"

Damon waved him inside. "Sure. Come on in."

Zep closed the door behind him after he stepped inside, as if he didn't want to chance their conversation being overheard. The move had Damon's brow furrowing.

"Is everything okay?"

Even though Zep nodded, he still looked nervous. He worried at the hem of his t-shirt, making

Damon nervous just looking at him. "It's about Lucky."

The hair on the back of Damon's neck stood. His shoulders tensed. "What about him?"

Zep twisted his hem again. "Well, you know how we take a cooking class together?"

Damon nodded, unsure where this was headed. "He told me about it."

Zep's spine visibly stiffened and he looked suddenly determined. "I don't think it's safe for Lucky to live upstairs."

Damon's stomach muscles clenched with dread. "Tobin lived upstairs for years without any problems."

"I know," Zep said with a nod. "But Lucky isn't Tobin. Tobin may be a tiny thing, but he's fierce. He would have gutted any man who tried hurting him. Lucky is way too trusting to be so pretty. Not that I think any of the regulars here would do anything," he rushed to add. "But lately, there's been more and more strangers showing up when Lucky works nights. Even when we come home from our cooking classes, they're waiting for him. Sometimes, they follow him all the way up the stairs, harassing him for attention until he shuts the door in their faces. You've done an outstanding job of keeping this place as a fun and safe space, but Lucky isn't safe here. He isn't like most people."

Damon wanted to ask what Zep meant, and pretend he didn't understand, but he did. It was like Lucky didn't possess something everyone else was born with. Some natural sense of self-preservation had been stripped from him as a child. He wanted people to like him. No matter the cost or how terrible the person was, Lucky wouldn't protect himself because he couldn't stand the thought of upsetting anyone. Lucky needed a constant and loving protector.

"Thanks, Zep. None of that has occurred to me, but you're right. Lucky shouldn't be here at night alone. I appreciate you looking out for him. I'll talk to him and get something figured out."

Zep's shoulders sagged, as if a weight had been lifted from them. "I appreciate it, Damon. You're a good man. I figured you'd want to know."

Damon forced a smile to his lips as Zep left him alone. Zep was the one who was a good man. Damon was just a guy in love with a much younger man. No matter his reasons for needing Lucky safe, Damon wouldn't let anyone harm Lucky. The more Damon thought about Zep's claims, the angrier he became. Let him see some bastard following his man all the way upstairs, harassing him. That dude wouldn't walk again.

Damon shot to his feet and headed for the door. He stopped inside the doorway and leaned against its frame. Damon watched while Lucky poured drinks. He smiled and chatted. Men leaned farther over the bar than necessary, hanging on his every word. Damon knew Lucky well enough to know Lucky was clueless to their lust. He just wanted so badly to be everyone's friend. Damon headed back to his desk and started making calls. First, he found someone else to come in for the night. Then he went through several applications he had received through his website over the last six months. Damon scheduled three interviews for bartenders. He needed a new opener and a couple of floaters in case they got busy or someone called out. This place wasn't Lucky's responsibility. Damon needed to stop using the Road Clan as an excuse to keep Lucky around. He needed to get real and just keep Lucky the way he deserved.

With all that out of the way and Angelo here to relieve Lucky, Damon made his way back to the front. First things first; it was well past the time for Damon to publicly stake his claim. He hadn't intentionally kept Lucky a secret. They just weren't there together at the same time as the night crowd that often. Without slowing, Damon made a beeline for where Lucky stood chatting with a table full of regulars. Lucky's head turned Damon's way, as if he felt Damon's approach. His eyebrows rose, making Damon wonder what Lucky saw in Damon's expression. Most likely determination, because he was about to do something inside his bar that he had never done before. He closed the distance between them, snagged Lucky's waist, and hauled Lucky against him.

"What are you—"

Damon claimed Lucky's mouth, cutting off the question and answering it at the same time. He was marking his territory. Lucky's gorgeous body and face might be drawing in more business and making Damon more money, but Damon didn't give a shit. Lucky belonged to him. Only him. People needed to spread the word.

Damon lifted his head. He smiled at Lucky's dazed expression. Damon placed several more kisses all over Lucky's face as he walked him backward toward the door. "It's time to go home." As they reached the door, Damon pecked Lucky several more times until Lucky laughed, but he didn't try to get away. That said more than anything.

"Are you really doing this?"

Damon nodded and nuzzled Lucky's neck. "I'm damn proud you're wasting your time on me. Why shouldn't everyone know it?" Damon made his way outside without giving up his hold on Lucky.

He felt Lucky shrug. "Everyone will think you only gave me a job because we're sleeping together."

"Oh, sexy. They're not going to be thinking that at all. Now let's go upstairs and pack your things."

Lucky's muscles tensed. "Why?"

Damon backed Lucky against the wall next to the outside staircase. He didn't want Lucky getting away before he had his say. "I don't like sleeping without you. You're coming home with me."

Lucky's muscles relaxed, but his smile turned brittle. "Oh. You meant for the night. When you said to pack my things, I thought you were kicking me out."

Damon cocked his head to one side and eyed Lucky. "In a manner of speaking, I am. You're moving in with me."

The myriad of emotions that passed over Lucky's face in quick succession was almost comical. "Why?"

Damon knew he couldn't toy with Lucky. He needed to be in charge but loving. Otherwise, Lucky would retreat. "I told you. I don't like sleeping without you. So I've decided I won't anymore."

Lucky didn't immediately give in. "But you live a fairly good distance from here. I'll have to get up at like three thirty every day to get ready and be here by five every morning."

"I'm hiring someone else to do that. Until we get a new person trained, we'll do it together. We'll just have to be like old people and go to bed by eight every night."

Damon knew things weren't going well by the way Lucky turned even more crestfallen by the second. "You're taking away my apartment *and* my job. Why? Have I been doing a poor job around here or are you getting tired of me?"

Damon's heart tried twisting in his chest. He would never hurt Lucky. His heart couldn't take the way Lucky looked at him now. Damon felt like a puppy kicker. "No, baby. I'm asking you to put me out of my misery and move in with me. But I also know exactly what you pointed out about your hours. If you keep working mornings, you'll never get any sleep. So this is what I'm asking: move in with me and help me run the bar during my usual working hours. We'll come in whenever we get moving in the mornings and leave when we're done.

There are lots of times like tonight. Nights when I'm needed here for whatever reason. You'd still get the same number of hours, if not more, but we would be together more. Am I making sense or just rambling? I can't tell."

Lucky looked cautiously optimistic. His gaze moved over Damon's face. Damon could see the hope rising in Lucky's eyes. "So you're just saying you want to live together and spend pretty much every waking moment together."

Damon supposed he had said that. He wouldn't take it back. "Yeah."

An adorable smile touched Lucky's lips. "Okay."

A loud "whoop" escaped Damon before he could stop it from happening. He hadn't realized until Lucky agreed to his crazy plan how much he wanted this. Damon didn't want to be with anyone else. His heart had chosen Lucky when Damon hadn't been looking. He snatched Lucky from his feet and captured his mouth. As Lucky kissed him back, Damon found himself slowing down. Their kiss turned sweet and full of promise. Damon would take care of Lucky. Nothing bad would happen to Lucky on Damon's watch. It was time for them to start a new phase in their lives. Lucky needed to learn how to be properly loved. Damon needed to open his heart again. This was a good start. They would be perfect together.

INSIDE, LUCKY JUMPED UP AND DOWN LIKE A KID who had eaten too much sugar. He couldn't believe Damon wanted to move in together. That was insane. It was beautiful. Damon hadn't said he loved Lucky, and Lucky didn't expect Damon ever would. That didn't matter. They were going places and Lucky was in love with Damon.

"We should go upstairs and enjoy my bed one last time."

Damon hummed against the side of Lucky's neck. "You don't have to twist my arm. I'm always ready to take you to bed. We can pack your things in the morning."

"Goddamn, Lucky. I've been texting you all night and you're hiding in the shadows."

Lucky startled at Kit's sudden appearance.

Damon rubbed Lucky's arms, as if trying to soothe him.

Kit barreled their way. He wore a bright smile despite his complaint. "Don't you check your phone?"

"I keep it turned off while I'm working. What did I miss?"

Kit practically levitated in his open excitement. "We've gotten an offer for a movie. This guy saw our spread and he says we're exactly the gay couple he's been looking for to star in his upcoming Christmas movie."

There was no way Lucky heard right. "Are you kidding me? What kind of Christmas movie?"

Kit bounced, obviously incapable of holding back a second longer. "It's one of those cutesy things. You know the ones. Like, a bumbling baker meets a lumberjack who brings him a tree for Christmas or some shit. This is a big fucking deal, Lucky."

Lucky sucked in a sharp breath. He couldn't believe this was happening. "Holy shit." His gaze slid Damon's way.

Damon wore an enormous smile. "I'm super proud of you, baby."

A shout escaped Lucky before he could stop it from happening. Kit leapt into Lucky's arms. Before he knew what was happening, Damon had them in a group hug.

"Drinks on me," Damon said, steering them toward the door. "Let's celebrate while Kit fills in all the details."

"Oh. Oh," Kit repeated like a skipping record. "I forgot the best part. Filming is right here in L.A., so we'll be sleeping in our own beds every night too."

Lucky couldn't stop smiling. This had been the best night of his life. He didn't know why, but this felt like Damon's doing. Lucky didn't think Damon had literally gotten him the part. It was more like Damon had given him a steady life so Lucky could wait for better things to happen to him. This felt like the beginning of a new life. He couldn't wait to see what happened next. For once, Lucky had hope. He almost didn't recognize the feeling in his chest. It felt like pride. Damn. Lucky could get addicted to this. His gaze slid toward Damon. Their gazes met. Lucky nearly cried. Damon was the best person Lucky had ever met. He wanted to keep him forever.

SEVEN

FOUR MONTHS PASSED in a blink of an eye. Filming was slowly coming to an end and Lucky had been too busy to breathe. Even though he worked in the same town where he lived, Lucky felt like he never got to spend time with Damon any longer. It seemed the moment Kit and he signed their contracts, they had been tossed into filming. Lucky found himself scraping for any time at all with Damon. His role paid seventy-five thousand, which was more than Lucky had ever made in his life at one time. Since Damon had been taking care of him, Lucky also still had most of the money he had made from the magazine spread. Lucky planned to take Damon on a nice vacation, and he hoped to buy an old muscle car Damon had his eye on. He had never gotten to spoil anyone before. Damon deserved to have someone buying him things. The idea of surprising Damon with that car kept Lucky going through the late nights of filming. Tonight seemed especially bad. Lucky felt off for some reason. He wanted to go home. His phone buzzed.

Damon: *Hey sweet baby. How's work going?*

A smile tugged at Lucky's lips. He bit his bottom lip, hoping to hide his reaction. The last thing Lucky wanted was to look crazy while staring at his phone.

Lucky: *I was just sitting here missing you.*

Damon: *Just sitting there? Does that mean you'll be on your way home soon? **hopeful face***

Lucky: *Unfortunately, no. Kit is finishing up a scene and then we have one more thing to do together before we can go. It's probably at least two more hours before I can leave.*

Damon: *That makes me sad, but I understand. This is your dream and I support you. But I also miss you.*

After reading Damon's message, Lucky stared at the device and turned Damon's words over in his head. He wasn't so sure this was his dream anymore. Kit claimed Lucky was special and wasn't born for a normal life. Lucky still wanted this, but he wanted Damon more. Working all the time made him feel like he missed out on something even better. Sooner or later, Damon would get bored with Lucky never being home. The sick feeling in his gut grew. He wanted to go home.

"Are you ready to head home?"

Lucky looked up from his phone. Kit stood waiting for his attention. "I thought we had another scene tonight."

Kit shrugged. "They decided to do it tomorrow. I figured you would be more excited to get home to Damon than this."

Without a single care for pride, Lucky jumped to his feet. "Yes."

A bright smile lit Kit's face. "That's more like it." He linked arms with Lucky as they headed for the parking lot. "I have to say, when you first started dating this guy, I wasn't too sure about him. He looked a little too rough and tumble for you. But I like him, and you know I don't like many people."

That was some high praise coming from Kit. Lucky tried not to beam like a pride-filled idiot. "It's crazy. I've never been this happy. In the past, I've just sort of stayed with people until they put me out. I always knew that it was their house and I was temporary." He glanced over and met Kit's stare.

"This doesn't feel the same. It's our house. This feels permanent."

"Awww. I'm so happy for you, Lucky. No one deserves a happy life as much as you do. Plus, he supports you in your dreams. Guys like Damon don't come around every day. It's like you two are meant to be. That's so sweet."

"What about you?" Lucky asked, trying to turn the subject from himself. He felt like he talked too much about Damon. Kit had to hear about him all the time. It was Kit's turn to spill.

He felt Kit shrug. "Meh. You know me. I like my own company until I don't. Believe it or not, Zep and I have still been hanging out. Just as friends, obviously. Still no chemistry there, but he's smart, nice, and very pretty to look at, so there's that."

"He is all of those things, for sure. I'm glad you're still talking to him. I feel terrible about having to quit our cooking classes. Between this, the bar, and Damon, there were zero hours in the day for one more thing."

Kit unlocked the car. He didn't respond until they were inside. "Zep understands. He really doesn't have a lot of free time these days either. It seems like every celebrity in L.A. decided to get pregnant at the same time. Plus, he's a big softy on the inside. He's a sucker for your love story."

Lucky laughed, but he didn't mean it. Kit's final claim had a hint of sadness rearing its head. That was the one thing missing in Lucky's life. Damon didn't actually love Lucky. They were happy, and—like Lucky said—they felt permanent, but Damon never claimed to love Lucky. Lucky was sickeningly in love with Damon, but he kept the words to himself. He didn't want to say them and make things awkward when Damon couldn't say them back. Damon treated Lucky like a king. It would have to be enough. Lucky couldn't let himself get discontented. Sometimes... well, almost always, Lucky was his own worst enemy. He couldn't let that become the case with Damon. They were happy. This was better than love. They were content. Contentment was the thing that carried people through the years. Lucky could settle for that. It wasn't like he had any other choice. Damon didn't love him. It wasn't like Lucky could force Damon to love him and it was likely Damon never would feel the same as Lucky. Lucky just needed to accept things as they were. How depressing.

DAMON HATED THE NIGHTS WHEN LUCKY worked late. He knew Lucky currently lived his dream, so Damon kept his loneliness to himself, but he wanted Lucky to get home already. Damon found himself pacing the floor and watching the clock. He fought the urge to text Lucky again and ask what time he would be home. After all, he had texted him that same question literally ten minutes ago. It was possible he was the tiniest bit sickeningly in love with Lucky. He was also whipped. All Damon wanted was to sit on the couch and hold Lucky's hand. For some reason, he was twice as desperate for Lucky's attention tonight. It felt like Lucky would never get home. Damon's nerves were stretched to their limit.

The doorbell rang, cutting through Damon's thoughts. He didn't think Lucky would ring the bell unless his hands were full. Plus, Lucky had literally just said he had another scene to film. Still, Damon rushed to the door on the off-chance Lucky managed to wiggle out of work. He threw open the door. Frost stood on the other side. Damon blinked at the sight of him. They hadn't seen each other in nearly a year. Confusion had Damon slow to react. Frost flattened his palm against Damon's chest and pushed before following Damon into the house.

"Goddamn, sexy. Have you been working out? I swear you're bigger." He pulled his shirt up and over his head before tossing it aside.

Damon held his hands out as Frost tried closing the distance between them. It occurred to him too late that Frost didn't know Damon wasn't single any longer. It wasn't like they spoke anymore. "Whoa. It's been a while since I've seen you. I'm not—"

"Oh."

At the squeaked word, horror rose inside Damon. His head whipped toward the door. Lucky stood in the doorway with Kit at his back. Damon's gaze moved between Frost's shirtless state to Lucky's crushed expression and back again. Frost looked enraged by the interruption.

With a low growl, Frost bent and snatched his shirt from the ground. "Again, Damon? You're always blowing me off for your fucking problem child." He shoved his way out the door.

Kit hissed like a cat as he passed. "Oh, hell no. This motherfucker did not show up here to sleep with my best friend's man and then try to storm off like he's the injured party." Kit stamped after Frost like a man on a mission.

Damon couldn't defend Frost, even though this wasn't entirely Frost's fault. Damon had forgotten to tell Frost they wouldn't be seeing each other again, but it had been so long, Damon hadn't thought it necessary. The devastation in Lucky's eyes turned Damon into a dumbass. "It's not how it looks."

Lucky visibly took a breath. A sad smile touched his lips. "It's fine. You should go after your date."

His calm response broke Damon's brain. He knew how to deal with anger, and he understood Lucky when he was on the verge of a panic attack. This was different. It was a sad acceptance.

Lucky made a helpless gesture. "I'm no one. Everyone cheats, but I don't want to be the reason your date thinks that you do."

Damon couldn't breathe. He felt like he was dry drowning. Lucky had visibly retreated, shielding his heart from more damage. A shiver ran down Damon's spine. Lucky suddenly looked frighteningly familiar to Damon. He had the same emptiness in his eyes and tone that Mack had the day he killed himself. Lucky walked away. He was halfway to his car before Damon could make his legs work enough to scramble after him.

"Wait. Please, at least hear me out."

Lucky paused with his hand on his door handle. "You don't need to explain. You're not in love with me and I'm always gone. You should go after that guy before you lose your chance." Another weak smile touched Lucky's lips that didn't reach his eyes. "We both know that I'm just a pretty face. You should be with who you want." Lucky opened his car door—like he really planned to calmly leave, and Damon lost his shit. He could not lose Lucky the way he lost everyone.

"Would you stand still for five goddamn seconds and listen to me?" Lucky froze with one foot in his car at Damon's roared demand. Damon didn't waste time. He had to act quickly before Lucky's shock wore off and he got away. "That's the guy I used to sleep with before I started dating you. He works out of town and he didn't know I'm no longer single. Frost got here not two minutes before you and he started taking off his clothes before I could explain I'm off limits now." Damon closed the distance between them. "Look at me, Lucky. I'm telling you the truth. Please believe in me the way I believe in you when you're with Kit. I would never cheat on you."

Lucky wrapped his fingers around the top edge of the car door and dropped his forehead to his hands. His shoulders lifted and fell—like he tried desperately to hang on to his sanity. Finally, Lucky straightened and closed his door. He stamped toward the open front door and disappeared inside. Before Damon could catch up, Lucky re-emerged with the lamp Damon had given him as Lucky's first possession. Kit still had Frost cornered at his motorcycle, giving him hell. Lucky quickly closed the distance with Damon on his heels, hoping like hell Lucky wasn't about to land a murder charge. Frost glanced up as Lucky headed his way. To Damon's surprise, Frost quickly pulled his shirt back on as Lucky planted the lamp at his feet. "If you think you can take this lamp while on your bike, then you can have it, but that's all you're getting from my goddamn house. If you ever touch my man again, I will cut your fucking dick off."

Damon was speechless. He had never seen Lucky raise his voice or stand up for himself in any way. All Damon could do was stare in awe as Lucky spun back his way. He was terrified and proud as hell all at once. Lucky had called this place his home, and he still referred to Damon as his man. There was still hope. Damon had to cling to it.

Lucky pointed to the open front door. "You get your ass in the house and explain to me why this goddamn fool thought it was okay to come here and start stripping."

"I'm incredibly sorry," Frost said behind Lucky.

"I've been out of town and I didn't call ahead. So I didn't know Damon wasn't single any longer. This is entirely my fault."

No one paid Frost any attention. All eyes were on Lucky. He was a sight to behold in his rage as he headed for the door. It was as if he had listened to all he would hear from Frost. Once again, Damon scampered after him. He didn't know how much trouble he was still in, but he wasn't taking any chances by disobeying.

Lucky headed straight for their bedroom and Damon's anxiety spiked again. He prayed Lucky didn't start packing. Instead, Lucky fell facedown across their bed and didn't move.

With cautious optimism, Damon removed Lucky's shoes before crawling into bed beside him. He stroked Lucky's back. "I'm so sorry, baby."

"That guy called me your problem child," Lucky said with his face still buried in the mattress.

Damon swiped his hand across his eyes before going back to gently caressing Lucky. "I haven't seen him in a long time. So long, in fact, that I forgot he existed until he showed up. But back when we were..."

Lucky turned his face Damon's way. "Fucking," he supplied.

Damon winced. "Yeah, that. There were several times when I blew off plans with him to help you out or be with you. The last time we planned to get together was after Tobin and Sergio's wedding, but I went out with you instead. We pretty much stopped talking after that, and I didn't think about it one way or the other."

Lucky rolled onto his side and went up onto his elbow. "But I don't even know that guy. How would he know I'm the one you blew him off to be with?"

Without thought, Damon snorted. "Baby, you are absolutely beautiful. Everyone who has ever come to the bar knows who you are, even if you don't know them. When I said you needed me, Frost knew exactly who I meant. You're the angel God dropped at my feet."

A hint of a smile touched Lucky's lips. He dropped his gaze and stared at the bed. "I'm sorry I lost my temper."

Damon laughed. "Are you kidding me? That was amazing. I'm proud as hell of you." He touched Lucky's chin, coaxing Lucky to meet his gaze. When he had the gorgeous silver eyes that he loved so much focused on him, Damon let Lucky see his heart. "You are the love of my life. Don't ever stand for anyone trying to insert themselves between us. No matter the circumstances. This is forever, so that means we always have to fight for it."

"Do you love me?"

Damon's brow furrowed at Lucky's odd tone—like he didn't believe Damon meant it. "Of course."

"Then why haven't you said it before I caught you with someone else?"

For a moment, Damon was genuinely confused. "I thought you knew. You never tell me you love me, so I guess I thought you were one of those show don't tell people."

Lucky looked away. "It must be nice to be so sure of your perfection. I can't even begin to imagine what it must be like to know someone loves you to the point you don't need the words." His voice gave out on the last word, breaking Damon's heart. He hadn't realized he had been failing Lucky.

Damon crawled Lucky's way until he had Lucky on his back and could straddle Lucky's hips. Once he knew Lucky couldn't get away, he said everything he should have before now. "I love you." Lucky's eyes filled with tears. Damon was incapable of hardening his heart against it, but he kept talking. "If I'm not doing or saying something you need from me, tell me. I swear that I feel so goddamn deeply for you that you could demand anything. Hell, I have demands.

Like, I've wanted to marry you for a while now, but I'm scared you'll say no. So I just didn't say anything. Maybe it's time for us to speak up. I love you and I want to be your husband. You're amazing and I don't deserve you. I know you think you're an unfixable mess inside where no one can see. That's not true. You're just too good for this ugly world, but I want to be the man who protects you from it and holds your hand. How dare you think I don't love you?"

Lucky stayed expressionless through Damon's speech, except for his eyes. Lucky's eyes burned with passion. He snagged Damon's shirt with both hands and tugged, pulling Damon in for a kiss. A hairsbreadth from Damon's lips, Lucky locked down Damon's soul for good. "I love you too. Let's get married." He lifted his head and closed the final millimeter between them, claiming Damon's mouth before Damon could shout his joy. Somehow, Damon had gone from almost losing Lucky to winning the world in less than an hour. That was how quickly life could change, and that was why Damon had to get Lucky locked down right away. He couldn't live with losing him.

As much as Lucky wanted to melt down and fall into a puddle of self-destruction and pity, he had found himself being logical in a moment he would have fallen apart in the past. Frost still had his shoes on. That was the first detail that saved Lucky from wrecking his life. Not only was Frost wearing shoes, but Damon was completely dressed. Their bed was made. No one put their shoes on before putting their shirt on, so Frost had to be undressing not dressing. Damon had this sexy habit of unbuttoning his jeans just before he kissed Lucky. In those moments, Lucky always knew he was about to get fucked. Damon's jeans weren't unbuttoned. Lucky had chosen to trust his gut and match with his logic. Plus, he had been the one Damon chased after. Not Frost. That was why he had chosen to stay. Damn. He was glad he hadn't left, because now they were getting married. Unreal.

"Did you close the front door?" Lucky asked as he went to work on unbuttoning Damon's jeans.

Damon went still. A sexy chuckle rumbled from his chest. "I don't remember. Be right back."

Lucky laughed as Damon scrambled from the bed. While he waited, his mind tried turning against him. Had he stayed only because Damon chased after him? No one had ever begged him to stay before. Maybe Lucky was too easy to sway. Was he being an idiot? Blind? Lucky crossed his arms over his stomach, trying to protect himself from the darkness that pushed its way in. Frost was gorgeous. He had dark facial hair that begged to be touched and had some sexy as hell muscles. If Lucky pictured Damon with anyone, it would be Frost. Lucky hadn't been this close to a panic attack in months. He could feel it closing in, ready to suffocate him.

Damon reappeared in the doorway. His sexy red hair was already a mess and his cheeks were flushed. Damon's complexion made it impossible for him to hide arousal. Frost hadn't made Damon look like this. Lucky had. The panic gripping Lucky's throat loosened.

"I think Kit locked up for us." Damon's gaze moved over Lucky. "Nope. Don't you dare."

Lucky tried to pretend he didn't know what Damon meant. "Don't what?"

Damon crossed the room and started tugging at Lucky's clothes, peeling them away. "Don't you fucking dare start overthinking things. I can already see you forgetting everything we just talked about."

"Damon."

Damon froze at the sound of his name. He met Lucky's stare.

Lucky almost fell apart at the love he saw staring out at him. Damon was right. Lucky should have always known how much he was loved. "I love you."

Damon's features softened. "I love you too, baby."

"I don't want a big wedding. It'll only make me sad every time I think about how I have no family who would come. In fact, I don't even want to wait."

Damon nodded. "Okay. Let me take care of everything."

He would. Lucky trusted him. "Would you make love to me?"

Without a word, Damon stripped. Lucky's body tingled as every inch of Damon's large frame came into view. He was so fucking rugged and sexy. Damon had always worked out, but he had been going to the gym with Lucky too. Now he looked even harder than he had when they started dating. Lucky didn't care about that, but it definitely caught his eye now. Once nude, Damon went to work on peeling away the rest of Lucky's clothes. Cool air brushed Lucky's skin. When goosebumps ran down his body, Damon straddled him and used his body to keep Lucky warm.

Their lips met and parted. Their tongues played while their hands roamed. Damon found the lube that was always close at hand and went to work on readying Lucky's body while they kissed. Lucky let Damon do all the work, rearranging his body as Damon saw fit. With his eyes closed, Lucky focused on every touch. He memorized Damon's flavor while the anticipation built. Damon lazily pumped his oiled fingers inside Lucky's ass, massaging exactly where Lucky wanted him. A moan vibrated through their kiss as Damon slipped his crown inside Lucky's asshole. Lucky dug his fingers into Damon's skin and held on as the rest of Damon's dick stretched him wide.

Lucky tore his mouth away and gasped for air. He could barely breathe with so much pleasure vibrating through his body. Damon moved tortuously slow, rocking inside Lucky. The way their bodies moved with Lucky's cock trapped between them had Lucky barely holding on to sanity.

Damon open-mouth kissed every place he could reach while praising him between kisses. "You're so sexy, Lucky. I wish you knew how beautiful you are to me because I can see your heart. You're so goddamn blinding. I need you to have my last name. Maybe I'll still live in constant fear of losing you, but everyone will know you're mine."

Damon fucked with Lucky's head and his body.

He made Lucky believe he was important and loved. Unless someone knew what it was like to never feel either of those things, they couldn't understand what it was like to be with Damon.

"I love you, Lucky."

Lucky snagged Damon's chin and dove inside Damon's mouth with his tongue. He had to taste those words. Lucky needed them. He didn't stop kissing Damon as the pressure built. Damon was a dirty talker and Lucky loved that, but—tonight—Lucky needed connection. As he blew, Lucky cried out around Damon's tongue. Damon's muscles hardened. He thrust faster. His kiss turned biting and bruising. Lucky held on, riding the high as Damon plowed inside him. Damon ripped his mouth away and shouted as he came. He was so beautiful. Lucky couldn't look away. This man loved him. They would spend the rest of their lives together. Lucky wasn't alone anymore, and he wouldn't be again. Unfixable or not, he had found the other half of his soul. It was beautiful.

EIGHT

ZEP LIKED SITTING WITH LUCKY. He was peaceful. People weren't normally peaceful. They were chaotic and loud. That was why Zep always gravitated toward the quiet ones. The ones who had secrets in their eyes. Zep was by nature an observer. He liked to watch and puzzle things out around him. Zep had known the exact moment Lucky and Damon's relationship changed from friendship to more. He was also the first to notice the new band Lucky wore on his left hand. Zep nearly dropped his beer as Lucky passed it his way.

He grabbed Lucky's hand. "Holy crap. Is that what I think it is?"

Lucky beamed. "Yeah."

"When did this happen?"

Lucky glanced down at his ring before meeting Zep's stare again. "Filming wrapped on Thursday. We headed out to Vegas on Friday. So, three days ago."

"Wow." Zep couldn't stop staring at Lucky in awe. He truly had no idea how rare he was. Before him, Damon hadn't publicly dated anyone. Naturally, as an observer of life, Zep had noticed Damon leaving with someone here and there over the years. Damon hadn't given his heart to anyone. It was obvious now that Damon had simply been waiting for the perfect person to come along. Like Zep, not just anyone would do.

Kit reemerged from the bathroom and reclaimed his seat at Zep's side. "I see Lucky has been showing off his ring and bragging about cutting everyone out of his wedding."

Lucky rolled his eyes. This was obviously a complaint he had already heard a time or two.

Since Lucky wasn't one to stick up for himself, Zep accepted the honor. "I imagine Lucky wanted a private ceremony filled with peace and tranquility, starting his marriage off with the same tone in which he hopes to continue. You are neither quiet nor tranquil. I can't imagine why you weren't invited."

Kit punched his thigh. It didn't hurt, but it

proved Zep's point. Kit was a constant firecracker. He was exhausting. Zep wasn't entirely sure why he kept letting the guy talk him into doing things together. He supposed they were friends. That was the only excuse he could dredge up. When they had first met, Zep had been blinded by Kit's beauty and innocent appearance. Then they had gone on one date and Zep had quickly understood that—while still beautiful—Kit was not the same as Lucky. He was a bomb, ready to explode, and level everyone's life at any moment.

The door opened and Zep automatically looked that way. A groan rose in his throat. He quickly stifled the sound before it fell. Kit wasn't nearly as well-mannered at Frost's appearance, surprising no one.

"Well, look who it is. The homewrecker."

Frost's chest rose and fell, as if holding back an irritated sigh. Zep got it. Kit was a handful.

Lucky sighed. "Stop, Kit. It's fine. What can I get you?"

"Don't you wait on him," Kit fussed.

Zep set his hand on Kit's thigh and squeezed. To his surprise, Kit settled down. He hoped that meant their friendship had Zep rubbing off on Kit at least a little.

Frost held a lamp that looked like an old timey lamppost. He carried it around to Lucky's side of the bar and set it at his feet. "I stopped by the house, but you weren't home. I figured this would be the best place to look next." He motioned toward the lamp. "If you've got some place to plug this in, you'll see I fixed it for you. It just needed a new switch."

Lucky looked unsure of what he should do.

Zep leaned over the bar and moved a nearby blender, exposing the outlet behind it. Frost met Zep's gaze and flashed him a grateful smile. For a moment, Zep found himself mesmerized by Frost's light blue eyes. He had to force himself to sit down, but Frost's stare never wavered from Zep's. Zep had to take a steadying breath. This one was a sexual being. He likely broke hearts all over town.

As if taking his cue from Zep, Lucky plugged in the lamp and pulled all eyes the lamp's way. It immediately fired to life. For a moment, Lucky stared at the lamp expressionlessly. He visibly swallowed before meeting Frost's gaze again. "Thank you."

Frost shrugged. "It's no problem. I took some electrician classes after high school. It never actually went anywhere, but I guess some of what I learned stuck with me." He shifted from one foot to the other, looking uncomfortable. "Um, I know I have no right to ask, but is it okay if I talk to Damon? I don't want to step on any toes. I just need to explain and apologize. To you too, obviously. I couldn't be more embarrassed about what happened."

Lucky looked oddly fine. In fact, Zep would go as far as to say, he looked completely unconcerned about Frost in any way. Lucky nodded. "I know you didn't know we're together. He's in the storeroom if you want to head back there."

For a moment, Frost stared at Lucky, as if every bit as awed as Zep. Lucky was the portrait of class, and Zep was extra proud to know him in the moment. With a nod, Frost pushed his way through the door behind the bar that led inside the storeroom.

Kit lost his shit. "What the hell, Lucky? That guy already tried to fuck your man once. You can't trust him."

Lucky shrugged. "It doesn't matter if I can't trust him. I trust Damon."

In that moment, Zep finally saw the real reason he couldn't connect with Kit. Kit would never trust anyone enough to love them. For whatever reason, he possessed zero belief in the purity of soul mates. Zep wanted to love someone and be loved in return. He craved what Damon and Lucky had. Zep wanted marriage and kids. He wanted the whole shebang of growing old together and doting on grandkids. Kit would never want those things because he didn't believe they existed. They would never meet in the middle and end up together. Zep's gaze slid toward the storeroom where Frost had disappeared. Damn. Those eyes. Only an idiot would fall for someone like that.

———

DAMON HEARD THE DOOR OPEN BEHIND HIM AS he stacked the final box from this morning's beer truck in the corner of the storeroom. He was more than a little surprised to see Frost standing there when he turned. Damon's gaze automatically shot to the door that separated the bar from the storeroom. The last thing he needed was to get caught with Frost again. Almost losing Lucky once was enough for one lifetime. Now they were married. Under no circumstance would he hurt his marriage.

Frost made a dismissive motion behind him. "Lucky knows I'm back here. I asked his permission first."

That was oddly nice. Frost wasn't really known for being a nice guy. In fact, he had a very fitting name. "Oh." Damon didn't know what else to say. He supposed he should apologize. After all, there had been plenty of time for him to tell Frost he wasn't single any longer. Honestly, he had simply forgotten Frost's existence with Lucky always crowding his brain. Damon opened his mouth to say what he should have months ago. Frost didn't give him a chance.

"I don't really work out of town."

Damon snapped his teeth together. Shock stole his thoughts and made him stupid. He definitely forgot he planned to apologize. "What?"

Frost licked his lips, looking nervous. He rubbed the back of his neck—like a guilty child. "Yeah. Um, I own Fitness Titan Gym on the other side of town. I just didn't want to date you, but I still wanted to fuck whenever I had free time."

For real, Damon's brain was broken. He couldn't stop blinking and trying to catch up. It seemed like he should be angry, but he never wanted to date Frost either. Still, goddamn. That was a cold way to handle not wanting a relationship.

When Damon didn't say anything, Frost shifted

from foot to foot. "I fixed Lucky's lamp and gave it back to him. It was never my intention to ruin your life just because I'm not interested in sharing mine with anyone full time. I should've just told you that I only wanted to see you when I was horny and let you decide if you were cool with that. And I definitely should've always checked that you hadn't moved on before showing up. I'm not a homewrecker."

Damon seriously had nothing. Frost kept pausing—like trying to give Damon a chance to speak, but no words rose to the surface. He had dealt with cheats and liars in the past, but he hadn't expected this. The crazy thing was that he didn't even care. Yet it still kind of stung, which made zero sense. Maybe he simply recognized Frost had never even been his friend. They were nothing to each other at all and it was weird. Damon didn't understand how sex with Lucky could be so powerful and intimate while this guy meant less than nothing.

Frost chewed his bottom lip and stared at Damon. When Damon still couldn't think of a thing to say, Frost changed tactics. "What's the deal with the lamp anyhow?"

Damon cleared his throat. Even to his ears, it was

an uncomfortable sound. "It's the only thing Lucky owned before he married me."

"Oh." Frost blinked. "Wow. You guys are married. I really am the dick."

Five minutes ago, Damon would have argued. Now, he couldn't. Good people didn't lie the way Frost had. Damon's feelings weren't injured, but— eventually—Frost would definitely break someone with this bullshit. "Thank you for fixing Lucky's lamp and bringing it back to him."

With a nod, Frost shoved his hands in his pockets and eased toward the door. "It's no problem. I guess, have a nice life or whatever."

"Why did you bother with the lamp or apologizing? I mean, you could've just disappeared since I never mattered anyhow." Okay. Maybe Damon was a little pissed. He hated liars.

Frost shrugged. "The little guy out there really reamed me out. He had some shit to say, for real. There's a lot of anger in that one. I guess I never realized I look like such a dick until he pointed it out."

Damon didn't smile, even though he wanted to. Kit was definitely an explosive little thing. Damon was lucky to have Kit on his side. He wouldn't want him as an enemy. "Yeah. Kit is pretty protective of Lucky."

Frost nodded. "I can see why. He looked..." Frost shook his head. A sad smile touched his lips. "Let's just say that I never really saw myself until I saw Lucky's face when he came through that door. I'm not a good person and I'm okay with that, but I'm also not the type to go around intentionally crushing people. You didn't really want me either, so it didn't seem like a big deal. This mattered. Lucky didn't deserve what I did. I can tell he's a good person. You did good."

Damon nodded. He had done well. In fact, Damon would go as far as to say he had married his soul mate. He didn't intend to fuck it up. "It's been nice knowing you, Frost. I hope you have a great life."

"You too." Frost disappeared through the door and Damon stared at nothing for much longer than necessary. He still couldn't believe that Frost worked across town and created a whole fictional life in another town. It was insanity. Damon was damn glad to be married and out of this bullshit pool of dating. He felt sorry for anyone looking for real love. They were in for a challenge. A smile stretched Damon's lips. He couldn't be happier with the sweet angel he had been blessed with. In fact, he couldn't wait to get home.

Shortly after Frost left, Angelo came in to take over the bar. After tossing the guy a quick smile, Lucky went in search of Damon. He found his sexy husband, staring into space inside the storeroom. For a minute, Lucky watched him in silence. They were happy and strong. Frost couldn't break this. He was a bit surprised about the lamp. In a good way. He knew Frost didn't understand, but when Lucky had given him that lamp, he had literally traded all that he owned for Damon. Maybe, to most people, a lamp wasn't much. It had been all that Lucky had to give. He would gladly give everything away again and again until the end of time, if it meant he got to keep Damon.

"Is Angelo here already?"

Lucky nodded. "I had a thought. We should hit that all-you-can-eat ribs place again before we go home. There are no movie roles or photo shoots scheduled for the foreseeable future. I'm up to gain some weight."

With a smile, Damon crossed the room and

wrapped his arms around Lucky's waist. "I'm always up to consume some carbs with you. No doubt you'll have more roles than you can handle soon, and I'll never get to eat unhealthy again."

Lucky snorted. He loved this man. Life with Damon was calm, and Lucky wanted more. Damon made him greedy for more time. "What if I don't, though?"

Damon's brow furrowed. "What if you don't what? Eat unhealthy."

"Take anymore roles or gigs," Lucky said, feeling somewhat guilty even as he said the words. He knew he was blessed for getting as far as he had while other people would kill for even the small roles he had landed.

For a few moments, Damon simply stared at Lucky, as if trying to find the right words to deal with Lucky. Truthfully, this was one of the reasons he treasured Damon. Damon always took Lucky seriously. He never said only what he thought Lucky wanted to hear. Damon measured what he knew about Lucky against what was best for Lucky's future every time before giving advice. Damon drew an audible breath. "Were you happy doing the Christmas film?"

Lucky shrugged. "Yes and no. I liked working

with Kit, but I didn't love the long hours and feeling like we never saw each other. Also, I didn't care for the way some of the upper guys flirted too much—like I was for sale or something."

Damon's eye twitched, and Lucky pressed his lips together to keep from laughing. He knew Damon's jealous nature fought against his need to give Lucky solid advice. His voice was considerably tighter when he spoke again. "What do you think you would need to change to make you happier but keep you doing what you love?"

With Damon's questions in mind, Lucky turned the problem over in his mind. He didn't want to be completely dependent on Damon, because he wanted to make Damon's life easier and buy him lots of nice things. Lucky also didn't want to be away from Damon as much as he had been while filming. He needed balance. "I didn't hate the photoshoot. Kit and I work well together because we're like brothers. There's less than zero chance of anything sexual, even if I wasn't married. The photographer was female, so I felt super comfortable the entire time. Plus, I made a good chunk of change. I think, if I just stuck to picking up modeling gigs from time to time, I would be fine. That way, I'm not spending too much time away from you, but I'm still making enough money to spoil you."

A smile exploded across Damon's face. "Damn, baby. I'm spoiled as hell already. Just holding you makes me feel like I won the lottery, but I'll stand behind any decision you make, as long as you're happy."

Lucky fought a blush. For a guy named Lucky, Lucky had always been the biggest jinx. Then he had met Damon. Never in a million years would he have thought he would have been grateful for being pushed from a moving car. Looking at Damon made him believe it had been fate forcefully shoving him into the exact spot he was meant to be.

"I'm happy."

Damon shuffled closer and the air shifted in the room, turning heated. "Good. I'm thinking I should hide in my office with the man I love for a while before we stuff ourselves and need a nap."

Lucky's cheeks hurt from smiling so much. He couldn't believe this was how he would spend the rest of his life. Lucky couldn't ask for more. "It's a date." One Lucky would happily accept over and over again, for the rest of his life.

. . .

Keep an eye out for the next Candied Crush, *Beautifully Exposed*.

Please consider leaving a review at the retailer where you purchased this book. Reviews really help with a book's visibility, which allows me to continue writing more stories. Thank you, Charity.

ABOUT THE AUTHOR

Charity Parkerson is an award-winning and multi-published author with several companies. Born with no filter from her brain to her mouth, she decided to take this odd quirk and insert it in her characters.

*Eight-time Readers' Favorite Award Winner
　　*2015 Passionate Plume Award Finalist
　　*2013 Reviewers' Choice Award Winner
　　*2012 ARRA Finalist for Favorite Paranormal Romance
　　*Five-time winner of The Mistress of the Darkpath

Connect with her online:

—Sign up for my newsletter: http:// bit.ly/CharityNews
　　—Join my readers' group on Facebook: http:// bit.ly/CharitysTribe
　　—Website: charityparkerson.com

—Facebook: facebook.com/authorCharityParkerson

facebook.com/TheMenofSin

—Twitter: twitter.com/CharityParkerso

—Instagram: Instagram.com/sinnerauthor

—Bookbub: https://www.bookbub.com/authors/charity-parkerson

—Amazon page: author.to/CharityParkerson